POWER PLAY

Visit us at www.boldstrokesbooks.com

Praise for Julie Cannon

"*Heart 2 Heart* has many hot, intense sex scenes; Lane and Kyle sizzle across the pages…Cannon has given her readers a read that's fun as well as meaty."—*JustAboutWrite*

In *Heartland* "…There's nothing coy about the passion of these unalike dykes—it ignites at first encounter, and never abates… Cannon's well-constructed novel conveys more complexity of character and less overwrought melodrama than most stories in the crowded genre of lesbian-love-against-all-odds—a definite plus."—*Book Marks*

In *Heartland*, "Julie Cannon has created a wonderful romance. Rachel and Shivley are believable, likeable, bright, and funny. The scenery of the ranch is beautifully described, down to the smells, work, and dust. This is an extremely engaging book, full of humor, drama, and some very hot, hot sex!" —*JustAboutWrite*

By the Author

Come and Get Me

Heart 2 Heart

Heartland

Uncharted Passage

Just Business

Power Play

POWER PLAY

by

Julie Cannon

2009

Acknowledgments

I've been fortunate enough to work with and for quite a few successful women. Whether they knew it or not, I learned something from each one of them. What to do, what never to do, and everything in between. Tate and Victoria aren't based on any one woman, but they do carry characteristics of just about everyone I know.

Dedication

To all the women in the C suite, and those who aspire to be.

CHAPTER ONE

I want this company, Monroe."
        Tate sat quietly, determined not to let her boss see how angry she was.

"I don't want any excuses and I won't accept anything other than Braxton's head on my table and his company in my pocket." The old man slammed his fist on the table, practically shouting the last few words.

What burr had gotten up his butt? Who did he think she was? Some fresh-out-of-grad-school-newbie with wet ink on her diploma and an imitation alligator briefcase? For God's sake, she was Tate Monroe, whose name caused more than one CEO to quake in his tassel loafers. She had worked beside Clayton Sumner for ten years after graduating summa cum laude with a Wharton MBA and a Coach briefcase. She always delivered exactly what he wanted, and it pissed her off that he would think that she wouldn't this time.

"Clayton," Tate tried to keep her tone neutral, "have I ever failed to deliver something you wanted?" Her question was rhetorical. "Everyone knows Braxton is a perfect fit for Sumner, including Peter Braxton himself. What's there to discuss? We'll make him a decent offer and he'll gobble it up."

"You bring this in for me, Monroe, and you'll be the next CEO of Sumner Enterprises."

Tate snapped up her head and fought for control. Clayton hated any show of emotion, whether it was anger, disappointment, joy, or excitement. Tate had learned early on to master any outward sign of what she was feeling.

"You heard me. I'm tired of all this shit. Time for me to ride off into the sunset and grab me some bootie on the warm beaches of Tahiti next summer. I don't trust any of those bean counters that work for me. I know I can count on you to keep Sumner and *me* in cash."

Clayton was a chauvinist but that didn't matter. Tate knew she initially got the interview because he thought she was a man and suspected she got the job because she was a lesbian. He had always treated her as one of the guys.

"But I don't want to pay Braxton one red cent more than I have to."

Tate was still elated over his promise to make her CEO, and soon. She hadn't thought he'd be ready to retire for at least another five or six years. She shook her head and glanced around Clayton's office. He had certainly decorated the expansive room lavishly. Every piece of furniture was custom-made, the art work original, and the plush carpet so thick that her shoes sank into it every time she entered.

"When I get through with Braxton, he won't know what hit him. He'll think he's just made the deal of the century, but he'll barely come out with enough money to pay his bills. Don't worry. I'll take care of it." She rose from the Queen Anne chair.

"See that you do."

Tate walked out of Clayton's office and crossed the hall to her own. It was the first week in August, so the sun was high in the sky, and light hit her from all directions. She didn't sit down at her desk but stood with her back to the room and gazed out the floor-to-ceiling windows that flanked her office.

As a child she had dreamed of having a job with an office instead of being a common laborer at the paper factory like practically everyone else in her hometown of Hillsdale, Georgia. Her father had worked there from age sixteen, along with his two brothers and their father. Her mother was a housewife who spent most of her time dodging her husband's fists and bill collectors, and drinking herself into oblivion. Tate was a long way from Hillsdale now. She had studied and worked and clawed her way to where she was now, and her feet itched to take the final step.

Tate spun her leather chair toward her computer, sat down, and began to tap the keys. Soon she found what she was looking for and hit the Print button. Page after page of information on Braxton Products spilled out of the printer, neatly filling the bottom inch of the output tray. While the printer chugged, Tate picked up the phone and dialed the one man who would know everything possible about the company that would make her a star.

"Max, it's Tate," she said after the voice mail beeped. "Hey, I need everything you have on Braxton Products. Financials, client base, customer lists, employee information, everything, including the dirt." Tate paused. "Especially the dirt. I want to know who is hiding what skeleton and where the key to the closet is. I need this ASAP, dude, so price is no object." She hung up. The thrill of the chase began to pulse through her veins and she knew just how to celebrate.

❖

"Victoria, we *need* this company. The board is getting restless."

"I know, Edward. I've received several phone calls this week. It's all Albert can do to keep the vultures at bay." Victoria Sosa didn't need anyone to tell her how desperately they needed this merger. As the CEO of Drake Pharmaceuticals she knew everything about the company, from the name of the mail clerk to the price of the compounds that made up their best-selling antiseizure drug. She could recite their financials in her sleep, and lately she had. She met with her chief financial officer three times a week, and the numbers kept getting redder.

"Victoria, some of the board members think it might be time for a new direction."

Victoria's heart skipped but she remained calm. "You mean a new *leader*, don't you, Edward?" This was not news to her. She had been down this road before with some of her peers. *A new direction* was a euphemism for *you're fired*. She watched the chairman of her board struggle with a response. "Relax, Edward. I know what I'm up against. I'm confident we can come to terms with Braxton Products. Their inventory fits the hole we have in our supply chain, their customer base practically mirrors ours, and their culture is very similar. When Peter Braxton sees that we'll let them be a stand-alone business unit he'll be thrilled. I have a meeting with him next week."

"Victoria, you realize I have complete faith in you—"

"And I appreciate that, Edward. The people working for me are great, and they're committed to making this merger happen." Victoria had either handpicked or personally groomed her senior staff and would defend their ability and dedication to the very end. She just hoped the end wasn't looming just around the corner.

Edward left, giving Victoria a few minutes to reflect on their conversation before her next meeting began. She had been the CEO for eight years, and during that time the pharmaceutical industry had taken a huge hit from Wall Street. Investor confidence was at an all-time low, and the FDA had dug in its heels on several patents Drake had pending. All in all the company had fought one battle after another. She sighed and straightened as her CFO entered her office, wearing her familiar worried expression. Victoria had one fight left in her, and hopefully acquiring Braxton Products wasn't the one that would cause her demise.

CHAPTER TWO

Any questions so far?" Victoria glanced around the conference table at her direct staff. The company's head of research and development, the vice president of human resources, head of marketing, her administrative assistant, and Robert Moore, the chief legal officer, looked as if they were in a pre-flight briefing. Her chief financial officer and longtime friend, Claire McCarty, sat at the end of the oval table. A brunette with unrelenting drive, Claire drummed her fingers on the walnut table in time to the rocking of her chair, her papers spread out in front of her in neat little piles, her calculator at the ready. The company could not be successful without these six people.

A major headhunting firm had recruited Victoria Sosa to run Drake eight years ago. At thirty-six she became one of the youngest CEOs of a Fortune 500 company in the country, and she had carefully built her staff around her. Working together as a team of strong personalities, they knew each other's strengths, weaknesses, and foibles. Their discussions often became heated and animated, but they respected each other's opinions and supported one another. They were also unafraid to question Victoria's decisions, and she valued their input.

"Okay. The board is counting on us to bring Braxton in. Contrary to word on the street, this deal is not about me or my continued seat at the head of this table. It's about Drake. It's always about Drake and keeping the values and services that this company provides to millions. We provide healthcare services to the neediest population when other companies don't think they can profit enough from them. We cannot let these people down." Everyone around the table nodded, even if they had heard this speech a hundred or a thousand times.

James Drake, a Harvard-educated PhD who founded Drake forty-two years ago, believed that researchers should be adequately funded to discover a cure for all diseases, not just those where money could be made. The big pharmaceuticals shunned "orphan drugs."

"Okay, let's go around and get all we know about Braxton out on the table."

Victoria admired the detail and thoroughness of the information her staff provided for the next three hours, jotting down occasional notes to remind herself of something or to clarify a point. She made additional notes as each person presented, intending to coach them in areas they could improve on. Her job was not simply to run the company, but to mold the leaders that would follow her. She didn't plan to leave, but she wanted to ensure that if she did, someone could fill her shoes without disrupting Drake.

She looked up from her notes when Claire finally stopped spouting numbers and mentioned the name Lisa Billings. Lisa was a senior vice president for the investment-banking firm Drake had hired to help them secure not only the financing they would need to buy Braxton, but confidential information and analysis on Braxton.

Victoria and Lisa recognized each other as lesbians the minute they shook hands. Lisa was tall and attractive with short, jet black hair that framed her oval face. Her eyes, equally dark, were sharp and focused when she spoke. Her suits were impeccable and fashionable, equally a badge of status with Tollison Brothers, her firm.

They met for the second time over dinner at the posh La

Boheme restaurant in midtown Manhattan, not far from the Tollison offices and across the street from Victoria's hotel. She had come to New York to meet with several investment bankers to secure the funding Drake so desperately needed. Over the best steak she had had in a long time, Lisa asked some perfunctory questions about Victoria's personal life, but Victoria always pulled them back to business topics. Lisa was attractive, and at another time and under other circumstances Victoria might have ventured down the personal path, but now she was fighting for Drake's life. She couldn't afford to be distracted.

"Lisa's coming to town next week to brief us on the latest information Tollison has gathered on Braxton," Claire was saying. "Victoria, she's already on your calendar for Tuesday afternoon."

"Ms. Sosa, do you want me to arrange dinner for you two Tuesday evening?" Albert Heard, Victoria's administrative assistant, asked.

Albert, who was fifty-eight years old, was the most polished administrative assistant she had ever had. He was British and very proud of his role as her gatekeeper and protector. Though she told him repeatedly he didn't need to be so formal with her, he simply replied that he took his job seriously and was proud she had selected him. It was not in his nature to be anything other than professional, he said.

"Yes. Albert, thank you." Victoria had a nagging thought that she already had plans for the evening. It wouldn't be the first time she canceled personal plans for business and would definitely not be the last. Albert would remind her later of whatever it was.

"Okay, everybody." Victoria closed her notebook. "You know what we need to do. I can't overemphasize the confidentiality of this deal. Until we have everything lined up, every i dotted and t crossed, we cannot let our interest in Braxton slip out. They are not looking for a buyer and won't like it when I approach Peter Braxton, their CEO. We have to be prepared. I don't expect any issues other than the normal, but we cannot be caught flatfooted.

We need this, and I'm counting on you to help me make it happen."
Victoria made eye contact with each staff member and saw the
seriousness of their situation reflected in each pair of eyes.

Shortly after the meeting broke up, Albert entered her office
carrying his standard steno pad and blue pen. One afternoon not
long after he was hired, she even saw him coming out of the
men's room with the pad under his arm and the pen in its standard
place, clipped inside the spiral.

"Excuse me, Ms. Sosa. You have tickets to the ballet with
Ms. Latile on Tuesday evening. Should I call her and cancel?"

At times Albert acted like her butler as well as her assistant.
He volunteered to run her personal errands, take her car into the
shop for an oil change, and reminded her to buy birthday cards
at least a week before the event popped up on her calendar. On
more than one occasion she wished she could take him home so
he could organize her personal life as efficiently as her business
life.

"No, thank you, Albert. I'll call her myself. Shit," she
mumbled under her breath. This was the third time in a row she
had to cancel with Carole. She would understand, but Victoria
knew how much she looked forward to seeing *Swan Lake*.

"Albert, send the tickets to her office. If I can't make it, she
can at least enjoy the performance." Carole had many friends and
shouldn't have any trouble finding someone to accompany her.

Carole Latile was Victoria's not-quite-so-serious girlfriend.
They had dated casually for a year, having dinner once or twice a
week, usually followed by equally enjoyable sex. Carole, the DA
for the city of Lake Forrest, a town just outside the Atlanta city
limits, carried a heavy workload and tried to be a surrogate mother
to her sister's kids, so she had as little free time as Victoria. They
enjoyed each other's company when they could get it, neither of
them pushing their relationship to the next level.

"Yes, ma'am. Will there be anything else?" Albert had his
pen poised to take down anything Victoria needed.

Victoria was about to say no, but he had assumed his puppy-dog look that said he wanted to do something to ease some of her burden. Instead she asked for a fresh cup of coffee. He jumped as if she had asked him to get the president of the United States on the phone for her.

Soon holding the steaming cup in her hand, she returned to reading the preliminary report that Lisa Billings had prepared on Braxton. She had been over it so many times she had almost memorized it, but each time she came away with an additional nugget of information or insight into the company. She and Lisa had decided they needed to completely understand Braxton and its CEO in order to pull off this deal.

Victoria always did her homework on anything she set her mind to. She was methodical by nature, knowing what she would do three steps before she had to do it. She was rarely impulsive, but preferred to plan her life as she would plan her business day. She would know this company as well as she knew her own before she even set foot in Peter Braxton's office.

CHAPTER THREE

Victoria shut down her computer and put several inches of paper into her Louis Vuitton briefcase. She had practically ordered Albert to leave at seven, and as she walked silently to the bank of elevators three hours later, she noticed that all the lights were off on the floor except hers. The scene was all too familiar. An early riser, she was often the first one in the office in the morning. But with Drake's recent difficulties she was now always the last to leave.

The elevator doors opened a few seconds after she pressed the Down button. She stepped inside, looking at herself in the mirrored doors as the elevator whisked her five floors to the lobby. Did she need a haircut or maybe even a new style? Her blond hair was still as full and shiny as it was twenty years ago, but maybe she was too old to be wearing it down, gathered in the back with a clasp. She had always heard that older women should have shorter hair. The style accentuated her high cheekbones and, other than the dark circles under her eyes, her perfect complexion. At forty-four she felt great and, judging by the second looks she got from men and women, she looked it as well.

Her house was not far from the office and the night was warm, so she put the top down on her convertible and drove home. Her heels clacked on the cement garage floor and, balancing her briefcase, purse, and a pile of mail, she unlocked her door that led from the garage into the house. After dropping the contents of her hands on the side table, Victoria kicked off her shoes and tossed her suit jacket on the chair. She didn't glance at it when it slid off the leather material and into a heap on the wood floor. It would be going to the dry cleaners with the clothes already piled in the seat of the chair.

Opening the refrigerator door, Victoria peered at the almost-bare shelves. Grocery shopping was one of her least favorite things, and it was obvious she had not forced herself to do the important yet mundane task. A carton of eggs sat alone on the second shelf, along with a block of cheese, a container of yogurt, and three apples on the third. Victoria reached for one of the beers that filled the top shelf, the eggs, cheese, and some ham from the crisper, and set to work whipping up an omelet.

Stomach full and finally relaxed she grabbed the phone and dropped into the sister chair of the one that was her temporary laundry basket. She pulled the lever, kicking up the footrest, and scrolled through the numbers programmed in her phone. She passed her mother, brother, two sisters, and Albert's home number, as well as the home numbers of everyone on her staff, finally stopping and pushing the dial button.

As the ringing sounded in her ear, Victoria looked at her feet and frowned. She desperately needed a pedicure and pulled her BlackBerry from her briefcase to make a note before she forgot. She had just finished keying in the reminder when a breathless voice on the other end of the phone answered.

"Hello."

"Carole? Are you all right?" It wasn't too late to call Carole. She was a night owl who rarely went to bed before midnight.

"I'm fine. I couldn't find the damn phone. The kids were over this evening, and when I heard the couch ringing I realized they obviously were playing with something they shouldn't have."

"How are they doing?" Carole's sister had died suddenly three years ago and she had stepped in to help her brother-in-law raise their three kids.

"They're great. Their dad is finally dating again, which is why I had the little cherubs tonight. Now I know why I became a lesbian. No way could I handle three kids twenty-four hours a day, seven days a week. I mean, I love these kids, but I am absolutely exhausted."

Victoria laughed. Carole often had the kids over to her house and always said the same thing after they left. "Makes my day sound like a walk in the park."

"You sound tired. What's up?" Carole was good at reading Victoria's moods and knew when to shut up and listen and when to probe.

"Remember a few months ago I told you we might have to acquire a company named Braxton Products?" Victoria continued after Carole replied yes. "Well, it's definite. I met with my staff today and we spent all afternoon working on it."

"Wow, Victoria. Should I offer my sympathies or congratulations? I know you viewed it as a blessing and a curse if you had to go down this path."

Victoria often talked to Carole about a problem or issue at Drake. A successful businesswoman herself, Carole knew enough to offer sound advice or no advice if Victoria simply needed to talk something through.

"Well, it's me who has to apologize. I can't make it Tuesday night. Our investment banker is coming to town and—"

"Don't worry about it, Victoria. I understand."

"Albert's sending the tickets to your office tomorrow. No reason you can't go and enjoy yourself."

"I said don't worry about it. I completely understand that business takes priority over your personal life in this case. I'll ask my mom to go with me. She'll love it."

The ease with which Carole accepted their canceled date troubled Victoria. Yes, there were those times when business did trump something personal, but lately they were becoming more the norm than the exception, and even though that didn't seem to bother Carole, it bothered her.

Her last relationship had ended two years ago when she walked out of a different house, tired of her partner Melissa's constant one-upmanship.

Melissa Vaughn's parents had spoiled her from the minute she exited the womb and were probably still doing so. Victoria had not seen or spoken to Melissa since she tossed her out of her office that ugly day seven months ago.

Melissa had marched into her office without warning when Albert was at lunch. She had been there frequently during the time they were together, often making derogatory comments about Victoria's furniture, paintings, or even the rain spots on the windows. By the look on her face, this time, Victoria knew, would be uglier than the last.

"How dare you treat me this way?" Melissa said.

Victoria put the cap on her Montblanc pen and looked across her wide mahogany desk, giving herself a moment to gather her thoughts. She was angry that she still allowed Melissa to rattle her. "What do you want, Melissa?" Victoria made a mental note to speak to the head of Drake security. She had warned him several times that Melissa might try to enter the facility and make a scene. She had been too quiet over the past few months, and Victoria knew her all too well.

"What do I want? What do I want?" Melissa paced in front of her desk like a Ping-Pong ball crossing back and forth over the net. "What I want is for you to show me some respect. That's what I want."

Victoria was not surprised when Melissa repeated herself. When she didn't have anything to say, she said the same thing over and over. At first Victoria found it charming. Now it simply annoyed her. "Melissa, I don't know what you're talking about. I treated you with the utmost respect the entire time we were together, and that has not changed since we broke up."

"*We* didn't break up, Victoria. You did."

Two years ago, Victoria had simply told Melissa she was not

happy with their relationship and planned to move out the next day. She had rented an apartment near Drake and signed a twelve-month lease, figuring that would give her and Melissa enough time to untangle their finances and property. Eight months ago she bought and moved into the house she called her own.

Victoria had met Melissa at a pickup basketball game. Not only was she gorgeous, but she was fiercely competitive. A win-at-all-cost woman. If she wanted something she had to have it and would not let anything stand in her way. She was successful in her own right, owning several high-end boutique shops that catered to the rich and famous in Lake Forrest. She was charming, persuasive, and had swept Victoria off her feet and into her arms in two dates.

It took Victoria almost two years for her head to clear from the mind-blowing, everyday sex. Then she began to see who Melissa really was. Being hyper-competitive, Melissa regarded everything as a challenge to her, and she *had* to win, whether it was who had the fastest car, the newest electronic gadget, or the biggest paycheck. In their personal life Melissa always had to have the first and last orgasm of the night and was never satisfied until Victoria had come at least twice. She seemingly had to prove to herself that she could get a woman off multiple times. In the beginning, Victoria had absolutely no complaints, but after she took the job at Drake, all she wanted to do most nights was go to bed and sleep.

Melissa had practically begged Victoria to take the job, and when Victoria figured out why, she was heartbroken. Melissa didn't want her to accept the position at Drake because Victoria wanted it or because it was the right move for her career. Melissa wanted a girlfriend who was a CEO of a major corporation. She wanted to parade Victoria in front of her friends and business associates, and more often than not, she did. One evening after attending yet another party she didn't want to go to, Victoria realized she was not happy in such a competitive relationship.

It took many more months before she finally had the guts to end it. She hated her cowardice and vowed never to be that spineless again.

Victoria refused to argue semantics with Melissa. "I'm busy right now. What do you want?" Not that Victoria planned to give her whatever it was. She had already given her enough.

"I want you to quit this stupid job and come back to me."

Victoria looked at the woman she had been with for seven years, feeling as if she had never seen her before. "What are you talking about? I'm not quitting and I'm certainly not coming back to you."

Melissa slowed her pacing. "Look, Vic. I admit things got a little strained between us when you took this job."

"A little strained?" Victoria shot back. "You call telling everyone you had hit the trifecta with your CEO wife, your third million dollars in the bank, and a new Bentley a little strained? You don't care about me, Melissa. I doubt if you ever did. I was just another notch in your belt. You have to be in competition with everyone for everything, and I was the grand trophy. I'm sorry, but I'm not interested in being a symbol on your mantle." Victoria's face burned with anger and embarrassment for not ending their relationship sooner.

"It wasn't like that, Vic."

Victoria hated that nickname. She calmly stood and circled to the front of her desk, stopping mere inches from the much-shorter Melissa. "That's exactly how it was, Melissa, and if you had any self-respect you wouldn't be in here begging me to come back. I don't want you or the life we had. Or the life you think we could have," Victoria added quickly, wanting to make it clear that they had no future. "Melissa, we are through, over, ended, whatever word you want to use to describe it. You have been less than civil to me through this entire breakup, and I suggest you leave before you make me really angry and I throw you out."

Victoria watched as Melissa tried to decide if she wanted

to stay and fight or do as Victoria demanded. Finally, after what felt like several minutes, Melissa spun around so fast Victoria could almost feel the air around her move. She stormed out of the office, slamming the solid oak door behind her.

"Victoria, are you there?"

Carole's voice brought her back to the present. "Yeah, sorry, what did you say?"

"It wasn't important. I'll let you go. Give me a call next week and we'll touch base and grab a bite or something."

Victoria didn't know if she felt relieved that she didn't have to maintain a conversation or disappointed that she didn't care enough to. Carole was a comfort. No pressure, no commitment, just whenever and whatever. Suddenly, in the midst of the most critical point in her professional life, Victoria realized she wanted more.

❖

The music was loud the way Tate liked it and her body pulsed to the beat of the bass as she walked through the crowded bar. The adrenaline from the afternoon still pounded through her veins and she felt invincible. At five foot six inches tall Tate realized she wasn't easily visible in the throng of women at the Left Seat, Atlanta's most fashionable lesbian bar. It was *the* place to be seen, and judging by the women practically standing shoulder to shoulder, every lesbian in town thought so as well. But the way Tate carried herself drew more than a few eyes her way. Some described it as a cocky swagger, others as confidence, and some simply called it "on the prowl." Either way, eyes and interest followed her and Tate noticed almost every one of them.

Tate was a regular at the Left Seat, preferring to meet women where she didn't need to spend much time or effort on small talk and the get-to-know-you conversations required in the other places she could meet lesbians. She didn't go in for the Sunday-morning breakfast clubs or the book-of-the-month gathering at the Book Binder or the numerous other social groups that filled Atlanta's gay-and-lesbian calendar. She was rarely in town. And when she was, the last thing she wanted was a connection any deeper than her fingers could go inside an equally willing partner.

She found an empty corner where by some miracle she squeezed into a space large enough to stand and watch the crowd without having her neighbors jostle her. Tate sipped her beer and lazily scanned the women on the dance floor, zeroing in on the uninhibited ones and those who appeared to be unattached. Women who were outgoing and unreserved on the dance floor were almost always equally unrestrained in the bedroom. She made eye contact with a slim redhead in jeans that were just tight enough to show off her ass and a green blouse cut low enough to display her other equally impressive assets. She smiled when the woman didn't look away.

❖

A week after her conversation with Clayton, Tate waited impatiently in the hard leather chair outside the office of Peter Braxton, CEO of Braxton Products. A distributor of medical supplies and equipment, Braxton couldn't compete with the big guys, Fraser Healthcare and Cardinal Health, but preferred to deal with the small clinics and doctors the major players neglected. Braxton prided itself on one-on-one customer service, but it had become increasingly difficult to be competitive with Fraser or Cardinal.

It had taken almost an act of God for Tate to get this appointment. First she had to get through Braxton's assistant, then convince the woman that she couldn't wait until the end of the month when "Mr. Braxton was available." The woman's snippy voice sounded again when she walked in the door. To make matters worse, Tate had been sitting in this uncomfortable chair for twenty-five minutes. She was about to say something to the woman, who had practically ignored her since she arrived, when a buzzer sounded and the woman stood.

"Mr. Braxton will see you now."

Tate didn't bother with a thank you but squared her shoulders and strode through the door.

The first thing she noticed was the size of the man's office, the second was the view of the Atlanta skyline, both of which were impressive. Braxton stood as she entered, his arm outstretched for a polite shake, but he didn't step out from behind the massive oak desk.

"Ms. Monroe, I'm sorry to keep you waiting."

Seemingly in his early fifties, he was well over six feet tall with thick gray hair combed straight back. He spoke with the customary Southern drawl and his handshake was firm.

Tate refused to say the obligatory "That's all right" or "No problem," because it wasn't. Her time was just as valuable as his and she wasn't about to let him think otherwise. "Mr. Braxton, I'd like to talk to you about a business opportunity." Tate cut right to the chase and sat down in the leather arm chair in front of the desk without being invited.

He settled in his chair and Tate said, "Mr. Braxton, I work for—"

"I know who you work for."

Tate wasn't surprised. Articles and pictures about her had appeared in the business journals frequently over the past few years as she successfully negotiated some of the largest takeovers in the country. "Then you probably know that we're interested in your company. We've studied your balance sheet, your P&L, and your income statement. Braxton is on shaky ground, Mr. Braxton, and we're in a position to offer you a substantial sum of money to help you out." Tate spoke confidently, expecting the man to react as all the other CEOs whom she approached with such an offer.

"Help me out or sell out?" Braxton asked calmly.

"We can consider this a mutual arrangement. You're teetering on the edge of a serious financial situation, and we can solve your problem, making you a very rich man as a result." Tate had a number in mind, a very large number that she would throw out if the discussion began to stall.

Braxton leaned back in his chair. "Whatever gives you the idea I'm in the market to sell?"

Tate chuckled. "Mr. Braxton, your business is failing. Your suppliers haven't been paid in months, the skyrocketing cost of fuel is eating through your dismal profits, and your fleet is growing older by the minute. If it gets any worse your investors will end up with pennies on the dollar, and I don't think they'd be very happy knowing you passed up a deal with a company as cash-rich as Sumner Enterprises." Tate kept her tone non-threatening but let her voice convey a knowing edge.

"And you think selling Braxton to you is what I need to do to—let's see now, how did you phrase it—help me out?"

"Yes, Mr. Braxton, that's exactly right."

Why wasn't he jumping at the deal? The noise on the street said the company's investors were ready for Braxton's head. This was a no-brainer. Sumner Enterprises' portfolio included a beverage company, several radio and television stations, eighteen utility companies scattered across the Midwest, and one of the largest publishing houses in the country. With such an eclectic range of companies Tate had never questioned why Clayton wanted Braxton. To her it was just another acquisition, but this one was her ticket to the top.

Braxton gazed at her for a moment before he spoke. "You present me with an interesting proposition, Ms. Monroe. I'll get back with you."

Reaching into her left breast pocket Tate withdrew a slip of paper folded in half and slid it across the large desk. The number on the paper in that pocket was substantially lower than the number on a similar piece in her right.

Braxton didn't even look at the crisp white paper in the middle of his blotter. His eyes never left hers, and it took Tate a moment to realize that her discussion with Braxton had ended. He didn't stand or even walk her to the door, but simply dismissed her with no more politeness than he would give the cleaning crew. Anger flushed through her veins and her face grew hot with rage. How dare he treat her like this? She was here to help him, and he had practically thrown her offer unopened back in her lap.

She stood and waited for a moment, controlling her anger before she spoke. "I advise you to take our offer, Mr. Braxton. It's the best one you'll get." She exited with as much purpose as when she entered.

Tate pounded the elevator button in the vestibule in frustration. No one had ever treated her with such indifference and disrespect as Braxton had. Was he suffering from dementia or was he a complete idiot? She was presenting him with more than a bailout of his struggling company. It was his retirement ticket. Correction, it was his solid-gold retirement ticket. Or at least it had been until she chose the paper in her left pocket instead of the right. In every deal she negotiated she came in with two numbers and often hadn't decided which she would put on the table until the negotiations were well under way. The same was true for Braxton. But when he practically insulted her, well, that was a "whole nuther ball game," as they said down here in the South. She could not lose this deal. Would not lose it.

She stepped in the elevator car and poked the button for the lobby. Her stomach dropped as the elevator swiftly descended the thirty-eight floors to the lobby level. She was still fuming as the doors opened and she stepped out, so incensed at Braxton's superior attitude she didn't see the woman approaching and walked right into her.

"Shit," Tate cursed, as the papers in the woman's portfolio scattered across the highly polished granite. The force of the impact knocked the other woman to the floor and forced the air out of Tate's lungs. She stepped back, inhaling sharply as proverbial stars danced before her eyes. "Goddamnit," she was able to say after her lungs refilled with stale lobby air. She had always had a slightly nasty mouth, especially when she was under stress. Like right now.

The woman on the ground finally caught her attention. Even sitting on the floor Tate could tell that she was tall, very tall, with long blond hair cascading over her left shoulder. She struggled to stand, her shoes slipping on the slick floor.

"Sorry." Tate reached out to help the woman up. A large warm hand filled hers and the woman was able to get some traction and stand. When she did, Tate found herself eye-to-breast with her. She had to be well over six feet tall. Tate had trouble raising her gaze from the enticing swell of the woman's chest, but when she did she met an expectant look from the clearest blue eyes she had ever seen.

Tate gawked at the woman, unable to do anything but. She was beautiful and graceful, even when she had sprawled on the floor like a rag doll. The woman wore an Armani suit the color of a cloudy sky, her contrasting silk blouse laying flat on the lapels of her dark jacket. Two diamond earrings winked from perfectly formed ears, while a small platinum necklace peeked out from the neckline of the blouse. For an extremely tall woman she was still feminine and sophisticated, looking like she just stepped out of a high-end fashion magazine. The woman's taste in clothes was far different from the J.Crew that filled Tate's closet.

The woman was apparently waiting for an apology or some other form of acknowledgment that Tate had knocked her on her ass in the middle of a public place. Several people rushed by, darting for the elevator before the doors closed.

"I'm sorry. I wasn't paying any attention. Are you all right?" Tate glanced up and down her body to make sure.

The blonde glanced at her watch impatiently. Tate stooped, gathered the papers, and placed them back in the woman's portfolio.

"Yes, thank you. I'm sorry but I have to catch the elevator. I'm late for a meeting." And with those few words she dashed into the elevator just before the doors closed again and transported its cargo to the many floors above.

Tate was still a bit winded from the encounter and her head hurt where she had connected with the woman's shoulder. Rubbing the spot, she exited the building with much more attention to her surroundings.

The vibration on her hip signaling a phone call took her thoughts from the tall woman, and the familiar number made her heart race.

"What've you got for me?"

Chapter Four

With a few minutes to spare before her meeting with Peter Braxton, Victoria dashed into the ladies' room just to the right of the elevator. Once inside she gave herself a quick once-over, making sure the collision in the lobby hadn't marred her appearance. Thankfully she wore her blue suit today instead of the beige one she originally had laid out. This one wouldn't show any residual dirt from the floor where she had surprisingly found herself.

At least the woman who had knocked her on her ass apologized and helped her up. All Victoria remembered about her were her bright green eyes and the feel of solid muscle hitting her like a linebacker. The woman hadn't even been looking where she was going when she stormed off the elevator. Victoria was lucky the collision hadn't hurt her.

Frowning, she examined her backside in the full-length mirror. She needed to renew her membership at the gym. She wasn't getting any younger, and at forty-four, she couldn't shed the pounds as easily as she put them on. She wore one size larger than she did in college and her weight had definitely shifted to different places. The finely tailored cut of her suit accentuated her positives and downplayed her negatives, and Victoria still garnered more than her share of appreciating eyes wherever she went. Most of it was because of her height. At six foot three she was definitely the tallest woman in the room, sometimes the tallest of *anyone* in the room, but people weren't just gawking at her height.

Pulling herself back to what she had come to accomplish, she smoothed and re-secured her hair in the tortoise clip at the nape of her neck, applied fresh lipstick, and with one last look in the mirror, she left.

The sign on the door spelled out Braxton Products in large Century Gothic letters etched in the frosty glass. She took a deep breath as she pulled and the door opened silently.

Braxton's reception area was furnished simply but elegantly in hues of blues and tans, with wide leather chairs banking one wall. Victoria's shoes tapped as she crossed the small area and stood in front of an empty desk. She casually looked to her left and then to her right and stepped back when she saw no one in the vicinity. Maybe the receptionist had slipped away for a cup of coffee or to deliver a message. Victoria waited patiently for several minutes before a harried elderly woman appeared from one of the unmarked doors behind the desk.

"I'm sorry to keep you waiting. How may I help you?"

Victoria smiled at the woman's polite tone. She had to be near eighty. "I'm Victoria Sosa. I have an appointment at ten thirty with Mr. Braxton."

The woman flipped a page in the appointment book on her desk. "Yes, here it is. His office is all the way down on your left. His assistant Susan will let him know you're here." She pointed in the right direction.

Victoria thanked her and gathered her thoughts as she walked down the hall. The doors of a few offices were open, and she heard the sound of voices in discussion and an occasional laugh. Her palms began to sweat as she neared the door marked Peter Braxton, President. Brushing her hand against her jacket she stepped into the most important meeting of her life.

Several minutes later, Braxton greeted Victoria with the reserve she expected and a look of anger she didn't. "Mr. Braxton, thank you for agreeing to see me." She extended her hand, which Braxton shook politely. He dropped her hand without returning her greeting, though, and Victoria felt awkward standing in the silence. Braxton looked at her critically.

"I'm sorry. Did I catch you at a bad time?" she asked.

After what seemed like forever, he finally spoke. "No, not at all, Ms. Sosa. Please sit down." He rounded his desk and offered her a chair in the sitting area of the large office. "May I offer you something to drink? Coffee? Tea, perhaps?"

Victoria was tempted to ask for some coffee. The cup, however small, would give her something firm to hold on to. She refused, not wanting any type of crutch for this crucial discussion. "No, thank you. I'm fine." She chose a straight-back leather chair while Braxton sat on the small couch. "Mr. Braxton, do you know why I'm here?"

"I have some idea, Ms. Sosa, but why don't you tell me so there is no misunderstanding."

"All right, but please call me Victoria." She smiled as she became less nervous. "Mr. Braxton, Drake Pharmaceuticals is in trouble." Victoria stopped to gauge the man's reaction, which was only a small flare of surprise in his brown eyes, then continued. She couldn't run away now, so she succinctly outlined the issues Drake was facing.

After several minutes she finally said what she had come to say. "If I'm not mistaken, Mr. Braxton, we are in the same financial lifeboat. I'd like to offer you a mutual lifeline. A merger. You have what I need and I have what you need. Together we can be successful. Unfortunately I can't offer you anywhere near the money another company can, but I can offer you this partnership. You have worked hard to make this company something to be proud of. You have an excellent business model but unfortunately have run into a bit of bad luck. I don't want your company, Mr. Braxton." Victoria paused for emphasis. "I want what Braxton can give Drake and what we can give you." She took the next ten minutes to outline her plan.

Braxton studied Victoria, then stood and walked the few steps to the coffeemaker that sat on top of the credenza. He raised a cup, offering Victoria coffee if she had changed her mind. When she shook her head he poured some for himself.

"Your situation is very interesting, Victoria. And call me Peter." He sat back down on the couch. "I had heard some rumors. But may I ask you a personal question?"

Victoria stiffened but didn't show any outward sign that she didn't want to discuss her personal life. She was here only on business. Far too many men and a few women thought it was okay to hit on her during a meeting. She was tired of it but chose the diplomatic way out. "As long I have the right to refuse to answer." She forced a light and unthreatening tone in her voice.

"Lady Bruins Volleyball, 1983?" he asked hesitantly.

"Excuse me?" Victoria had no idea what he was talking about.

"UCLA. You rallied from an 11-2 deficit to beat Stanford 15-13 in the fifth and final game of the NCAA championship match at Pauley Pavilion."

Victoria was stunned. It had been over twenty-five years since her freshman year at UCLA when she was the starting blocker on the championship team.

Braxton laughed. "My wife played for Stanford. Actually she wasn't my wife then, but I was planning on asking her to marry me right after the game." He looked a little sheepish. "I had fifty bucks on the Cardinal," he added, using the mascot name for the famed school in Palo Alto.

Victoria relaxed at his light banter and hid her surprise that a man Peter Braxton's age had a wife who was her peer. "I'm sorry we disappointed you and you lost your money. Did you go ahead and propose?"

"No way. Debbie was so upset she could hardly stop crying for a week. She took it hard."

"I can imagine. It was an unbelievable game." Victoria hadn't thought about her college volleyball career in ages and it all flooded back to her as if it were yesterday. She wasn't yet eighteen when she entered UCLA on a full-ride volleyball scholarship. The top volleyball player in Arizona, she had been heavily recruited by Stanford, Arizona State, and Oregon, choosing UCLA because of its outstanding business school. For five years she juggled classes, practice, games, and an occasional affair on her way to graduating summa cum laude in 1987. She had taken a year off when she was selected to be a member of the U.S. Olympic Volleyball Team.

"You were on the Olympic team, weren't you? The one that won the gold medal? Debbie again," he added at the shocked expression that must have been on her face. "Naturally she followed the games and wherever Debbie went, I tagged right behind her."

"Yes" was all Victoria managed to get out. When she stepped into Braxton's office she had no idea this conversation would occur. She thought for a moment and then a shadowy face popped into her head. "Debbie Winters?" She wasn't sure if she could recall the name of the player from Stanford.

"Winston. She was their setter for three years."

"Yes, Winston, that's right. I remember her now. Lots of red hair, always tied in a bun?" The face of Braxton's wife was becoming clearer now.

"Still does, as a matter of fact. Wait till I tell her we chatted today. She'll probably kill me. You *are* the enemy, you know?"

Victoria laughed along with Braxton. She knew the enemy he was referring to was the team that snatched the NCAA championship out of Stanford's hands.

Braxton grew quiet. "Victoria, your offer is tempting, but unfortunately I'm not the sole decision maker here, as you can imagine. I'll need a few days."

Victoria knew exactly where Braxton was coming from. She might be the CEO of Drake, but she was far from making the final decision in deals like this also.

"I understand, Peter." She rose from the chair and extended

her hand. "Think about it and let me know. Thank you for seeing me on such short notice."

He walked her to the door, and when he opened it he asked, "Do you still play?"

Victoria couldn't help but smile. "A few friends have conned me into a beach volleyball league. I've never worked so hard in my life." Of course she was twenty years older now and had always played on a hard court in an air-conditioned arena, not in the sand at the local park. But she didn't share that tidbit with him.

Five minutes and one handshake later Victoria leaned her head against the back of the elevator. She was exhausted. She hadn't slept much the past few weeks, especially last night, unable to shut off her mind because she was anticipating this meeting. She needed to relax, maybe find a pick-up game this weekend at the beach. Teams were always looking for players, especially someone her height. She shook her head. This wasn't the time to indulge in self-relaxation. Her company was failing and she had to do something about it.

She closed her eyes and her stomach growled as the car took her the thirty-plus floors back down to the lobby. She hadn't had breakfast, and when the doors opened she smelled the familiar scent of Dunkin' Donuts. Before she had a chance to open her eyes, a woman cleared her throat. A face she couldn't quite place was looking at her as if to ask, "Are you planning to get out or ride up and down all day?"

"Sorry," Victoria mumbled as she stepped out, allowing the woman to enter. She glanced around the building's lobby and quickly located the source of the delicious aroma. Stuck in the far corner was the familiar pink-and-orange sign, and she headed right toward it.

Chapter Five

Tate rode the elevator alone, her reflection frowning back at her from the mirrored doors. The woman standing in the car hadn't recognized her, but she was the one Tate had knocked down earlier in her anger to get out of the building. Her hair was a shade of blond Tate had never seen before but which reminded her of the sun. It would look more attractive down around her shoulders than cinched at the base of her head.

The woman was probably a soccer mom, Tate thought. With a husband in the Atlanta 'burbs, three kids, a housekeeper, she most likely brought her lunch every day in a brown paper bag and drove the car pool once a month. "God shoot me if I ever get like that," she said to her reflection, but her statement was pointless. She would never have more hair on her head than the current two inches cut short on the sides and sticking up all over on the top, absolutely zero kids, and wouldn't be caught dead even riding in a minivan. But the woman had the most amazing blue eyes she had ever seen. And did she ever smell good. Her perfume lingered in the elevator when she left. *Too bad.*

A ding indicated Tate had again reached her destination, and she shook off the memory of the tall, thin woman as she strode purposefully toward the receptionist she saw earlier.

"Good morning. I'd like to see Peter Braxton. I was in earlier this morning and need to talk to him again."

"Do you have an appointment?" the elderly woman behind the desk asked.

"I was in earlier," Tate repeated, "and just needed to step out for a minute. He said I could go right on back when I returned." Tate used the bluster she had learned from her boss. It always worked for him, and the look on the receptionist's face indicated it was about to work now. "Thanks," Tate said, dashing down the hall and not giving the woman a chance to say no.

Braxton's assistant wasn't at her desk, and Tate thanked God for small favors. Braxton was standing behind his desk looking out the large window. She knocked on the open door and entered the office when he whirled around.

"Peter, I'll only take a minute."

"I was under the impression our conversation was over, Ms. Monroe," he said sharply.

Tate chose to ignore the fact that Braxton was fuming. She had what he needed and he would just have to get over himself. "I think we parted on the wrong foot." She pasted on her most charming smile.

"And why do you believe that, Ms. Monroe? I was very clear."

Tate hesitated. A target had never treated her as coldly as Braxton had. Target, that was how she referred to the companies she and Clayton went after. Sometimes they masked them as mergers, some as partnerships, but this was an out-and-out acquisition of everything Braxton had. "*I* had the impression you didn't fully grasp the magnitude of what I am offering you, Peter," she said, repeating his phrase. "This is too important for Braxton for you to take lightly."

"Ms. Monroe, I don't take anything lightly when it concerns Braxton. I know exactly what you want, and I will give your offer the consideration that it's due."

Braxton's voice was eerily calm for a man on the verge of losing everything he had worked for. Tate was about to say more, but the look in his eyes told her not to. "My offer expires in one week."

❖

Victoria caught a dollop of filling on her finger before it landed on her blouse. The donut shop made her favorite, and as the chocolate-cream filling tantalized her taste buds, she kept wondering about the woman in the elevator. Why did she look so familiar? Surely Victoria would have remembered meeting her. Her shock of dark hair and blistering eyes were definitely her most alluring features. When she corrected herself to include the young woman's body in that description, a flash of heat shot through her.

The woman, probably in her early thirties, was dressed in what Victoria recognized as J.Crew, which made her feel old and dowdy in her Armani, however classic and fashionable. To be young, carefree, and confident again. Was I that confident at her age? A commentary ran through her head as she walked down the street to her car. So sure of myself and cocky. Am I still that way or have I become old and stodgy? Forty-four isn't old, for God's sake. I just feel old. She, however, acts like she owns the world. I used to feel like that, she thought. When did it change so that now the world owns me? Sometimes she wanted to simply chuck it all and work for a non-profit, get her hands *and* her brain involved.

Victoria arrived at her office without a trace of the white fluffy powder that covered the outside of her donuts as evidence of her weakness for sweets. She enjoyed a naturally high metabolism, and if she simply watched what she ate and indulged in her passion for sweets only once in a while, she could maintain her weight with not much trouble. I'll bet the woman at Braxton's office doesn't need to worry about what she eats. Victoria was surprised at the thought that crept into her head as she skimmed her e-mails.

The woman's face and hard body jumped into her mind like a bright idea. "That's where I know her from," she said excitedly.

"Who?" Albert walked in with the morning mail.

"I've been racking my brain trying to figure out where I knew this woman from that I saw this morning. Then I remembered. She practically ran me down when I got off the elevator at Braxton's office. She was coming out and I was going in and *bam.*" Victoria clapped her hands for emphasis. "She ran right into me. Felt like a brick wall."

"Are you okay?"

"I'm fine, just had the wind knocked out of me. When I saw her again after my meeting, I couldn't place her, but now I remember." Victoria recalled the woman as if she were standing in front of her.

She was much shorter than Victoria, but just about every female was shorter than her six feet three. Their contact told Victoria that the woman's body was trim and firm, topped off with spiky jet black hair. But Victoria was most aware of her eyes, which were the most vivid shade of green she'd ever seen. They were the color of fresh-cut rye grass, and when the woman had focused on her she recognized the intensity she had rarely seen in another woman's eyes other than on the volleyball court—an expression of single-minded determination.

Victoria put her briefcase on the desk and grabbed the stack of mail from her in-box. As she skimmed the pile Albert read off her appointments for the day, and she grimaced when she heard that the chairman of her board was on her calendar for ten minutes from now.

"When did he call?" The *he* she was referring to was Edward Hamacher III, the richest, crabbiest snob she had ever met. Victoria once wondered if Hamacher was born with blue blood in his veins or if he had a transfusion once he finally realized just how rich his family was. No one had probably ever called him Ed in his life, certainly never Eddie. In addition to being haughty, he was pompous, arrogant, and didn't like queers. He had said as much one evening after a dinner consisting of prime rib and several bottles of very expensive wine when he made her pick up the check.

"This morning. You didn't have any free time today but I squeezed him in." Albert sounded apologetic.

"It's all right, Albert." Victoria knew how persuasive Hamacher could be when he wanted something. She had been dealing with him for the past several years, and at times his holier-than-thou attitude was enough to send her over the cliff. He was the last thing she needed today and, by the sound of his voice already booming in the hall, the first thing on her agenda after returning from Braxton.

"Victoria," Hamacher said, walking into her office uninvited.

When he addressed her, his tone was always just this side of condescending. Of course she didn't have anyone to ask to confirm her belief, but in her gut she knew Hamacher didn't believe a woman should be running Drake. A trusted source said he was outvoted in Drake's selection of her as CEO, and she suspected he was salivating now that his chance to get her out was within reach. That is, if she didn't bring in Braxton.

"Edward," she said, "would you like some coffee?"

He settled onto the small couch in the sitting area of her office. "Yes, I'd love for you to bring me a cup. Milk, two sugars." He unbuttoned his suit jacket and draped his arm across the back of the couch.

The hair on the back of Victoria's neck rose as much as her temper at his insinuation that *she* would get his coffee like his secretary or, worse, a common servant. Albert saved her from calling him on his request by stating that he would get it. Hamacher almost sneered as Albert hurried out of the office.

"Good man you've got there, Victoria."

The tone in which he complimented Albert told Victoria that

Edward considered him anything but either good or a man. To Hamacher, the roles were definitely reversed. She chose to ignore that comment as well.

"What can I do for you, Edward?" Small talk was not in Hamacher's vocabulary so she didn't waste her time.

"Where are we with Braxton?"

Victoria knew he was here to check on her progress, but this was her office and she controlled Drake. She would make him ask for every piece of information he wanted. She sat across from him in a straight-backed chair, the one she normally occupied during meetings in this area of her office. She preferred to sit erect instead of slouch or appear to be sloppy, which was Hamacher's current position.

"I met with him this morning—"

"Is he going to accept?"

Albert set two steaming cups on the table between them, and Victoria waited until he left the room before she continued. "I gave him a general overview of our proposal." Victoria watched Hamacher's neck slowly redden.

"What do you mean, an overview? You led us to believe that you planned to present the full offer to him."

"With all due respect, Edward, you don't walk into the office of the CEO of a multi-billion-dollar company and just tell him you want to buy it and expect him to say okay." At times Victoria swore she was talking to a child.

"We don't have much time, Victoria."

Victoria translated his statement into "*You* don't have much time." Keeping her aggravation in check she replied calmly, "He would have thrown me to the curb. I'm sorry if you misunderstood what my meeting with him was about today. I intended simply to lay our cards on the table."

Hamacher frowned when she crossed her Armani-clad legs. Another one of his archaic beliefs was that women should wear skirts or, better yet, dresses. His wife probably had an entire closet of pumps and panty hose. She continued before he had a chance to patronize her again.

"Peter Braxton didn't ask me to leave his office, which I took as a positive sign. He asked the appropriate questions that led me to believe that he had not immediately disregarded my proposal. I told him to think about it and we'd talk in a few days."

Her hand was steady as she lifted the Wedgwood china to her mouth. The redness that had started on Hamacher's neck spread to the remainder of his head, not stopping until it covered every inch of his bald pate. He jumped off the couch and Victoria quickly stood, not wanting to have him tower over her. The fact that she was at least eight inches taller than him appeared to infuriate him even more.

"Let me make this perfectly clear, Victoria." He stepped closer. "You have sixty days to get Braxton's signature on the bottom line or *you are out*." He was so angry he practically spat. "Sixty days" were his parting words before he left her office as abruptly as he had entered.

CHAPTER SIX

T ate's cell phone rang as she walked into the locker room. Snapping it out of its case she glanced at the number, but instead of being pissed at the delay of her daily trip to the weight room, she smiled and flipped it open. "What've you got?"

The voice on the other end was succinct. "Braxton is sitting on major debt. I mean major. He has two outstanding loans totaling over one hundred million, and rumor on the street is that they are ready to call them in. He's a month or so, six at the longest, from having to declare bankruptcy. His suppliers are threatening to cut him off and one already has. The union is playing hardball with their contract negotiations, and the IRS is snooping at his back door. He has his ass in a sling and no sign of how he'll get it out."

"Who knows about this?" Tate glanced around to ensure no one was listening.

"The debt, everybody. The bank calling in their loan, no one, as far as I've been able to find out. The thing about the IRS is on the QT as well."

Braxton was on its last breath and she held the oxygen bottle to breathe life back into the company. She couldn't have anticipated it would be this easy. It would be like catching fish in a shallow pond. Tate smiled at her good fortune, then frowned when she realized she wouldn't have to hunt for Braxton, or maneuver, or jockey for position. She wouldn't experience the thrust and parry of offer and counteroffer. The thrill of the chase drove Tate every day. The ability to outthink the competition and ultimately take what she wanted was better than sex. Well, almost better. The ease of the Braxton takeover didn't lessen the thrill of acquiring it or the huge reward that would follow.

❖

"Shit, I'm late," Victoria said to her empty office. "Albert," she yelled. He stuck his head in her office. "Please call Claire and ask her to pull the SG&A expenses for the European offices and have her call me on my cell when she gets them." She tossed her portfolio into her briefcase. "Oh, and cancel my lunch date with whoever I'm having lunch with. I'll be at Braxton's."

The week since she had met with Peter Braxton had been more hectic than usual, and she seemed to be running a consistent ten minutes late for everything. The call from Braxton came at four fifteen yesterday, asking her to meet at his office today at ten thirty. By the time she got her car and battled crosstown traffic, she might just make it.

Victoria managed to reduce overhead expenses in Europe and talk to an investment banker during her forty-minute drive. She was used to multitasking and couldn't remember the last time she had simply driven her car with only the radio on. Other executives at her level had a car and driver, which enabled them to be more productive. She considered it a waste of money. She could drive her own car, for God's sake. After Victoria had one harrowing almost-accident while on a conference call, Claire had been trying to convince her to reconsider. Instead, she just paid more attention when she was behind the wheel.

Passing the Braxton building on the way to the parking garage, she could have sworn she saw the woman who knocked her down in the lobby last week. She must work here, Victoria thought as the woman entered the revolving door. She shifted her attention back to her driving and pulled into the garage.

The aroma of Dunkin' Donuts enticed her to stop, but however much she was tempted, this was not the time to savor a chocolate cream-filled donut. Ignoring the scent she crossed the lobby and waited patiently for the elevator. Her stomach growled, reminding her she had skipped breakfast and would probably miss lunch as well.

The elevator doors opened and Braxton's administrative assistant, Susan, stood waiting by the reception desk. "Good morning, Ms. Sosa. It's good to see you again. This way, please." The woman led her to a conference room halfway down the long hall. "Mr. Braxton will be with you shortly."

"Thank you—" Victoria saw that she wasn't alone in the room. The woman she noticed entering the building a few minutes ago was pouring a cup of coffee. She looked up and Victoria decided she must be on Braxton's staff and was here for the meeting. There was a flash of recognition when their eyes met.

"No ill effects from our collision last week?"

She was younger than Victoria remembered, but the same vivid green eyes were moving up and down her body as if checking for any residual injuries.

"None other than a little embarrassment." Victoria watched the woman's eyes make another path over her body, this time slower and more sensuous. She tingled where the green eyes traveled, but pushed the thought out of her mind. She was slightly insulted that one of Braxton's employees would so blatantly check her out. It was rude and extremely unprofessional. Victoria concluded that the cocky, brash woman probably used her charm and rogue looks to get away with this type of behavior all the time. No wonder Braxton's in trouble, she thought. This woman probably thinks that charm and sex appeal will run the business. Victoria usually let such things go, but something about the woman's insolent manner made her want to speak up. Before she had the chance Peter Braxton walked in, Susan trailing him.

"Good morning, ladies. Thanks for coming on short notice. Victoria, my wife says to tell you hello and she still hates you."

Braxton added a smile to his last words. He returned his attention to both of them. "I'm sure you two have introduced yourselves so I'll get right down to it. I've given both of your offers a lot of thought."

Tate stared at the tall blonde, stunned. *Our offers? Who is this woman anyway?* Tate had thought she was one of Braxton's minions sent to keep her occupied while she waited. She had briefly toyed with the idea of making a play for her, but she was older than the women Tate usually went out with. Maybe after she clinched this deal. She had given the old man credit for sending someone as attractive as this woman, but now she wasn't quite sure who she was. She also appeared mystified.

"This is what I plan to do," Braxton continued, apparently oblivious to the confusion in the room. "Since both of you want my company, I'm going through this exercise once. Susan here," he gestured toward his assistant, "will work with your assistants to coordinate everybody's schedules. We'll tour my operations in Chicago, Phoenix, Brussels, and Hong Kong. We'll meet together in every location, and at each one I'll answer any questions you have. During our trip, don't e-mail or phone me. At the end of your inspection you'll have time to develop your full proposal for the board and I'll make my decision then. Any questions?"

The blonde spoke. "Mr. Braxton, I'm afraid I missed something here." She faced Tate. "Who are you?"

"I'm the one who's going to take Peter's company right out from under you." Tate watched the surprised expression on the tall woman's face. *One point for me.*

"Monroe, don't be a smart-ass," Braxton bellowed. "Get used to this, ladies. We'll be spending a lot of time together the next few weeks."

Victoria sat in stunned silence as Braxton rose and left the room without saying anything else. Why didn't she know someone else was interested in Braxton? Of course there would be. Braxton was a well-run company that, through no fault of its own, had encountered difficult financial times. An earthquake in China eight months ago had severely damaged their major supplier's operation, and their banker had unexpectedly been placed in receivership. Their cash flow had dried up and the creditors were circling like buzzards.

Years of facing unexpected circumstances had prepared Victoria to recover from this shock quickly. At least on the outside. Her guts were churning and her stomach was lodged somewhere high in her throat. Shit, shit, shit, how did this happen? she said to herself, rising from her chair as the woman approached and held out her hand.

"Tate Monroe."

The woman's voice wasn't hard or edgy, as Victoria expected. In an instant they had gone from being strangers to adversaries, and Victoria had anticipated she would be cold toward her. But the voice she heard was soft and melodious, if not almost sensual. Victoria hesitated a moment before she grasped the outstretched hand in acknowledgement. "Victoria Sosa."

"Well, Ms. Sosa." Tate looked deeply into her eyes as if she were searching for something, the vivid green eyes becoming deep, dark, and intense. "May the best woman win." Tate held her hand longer than necessary, winked, and left the room.

Victoria inspected her palm. It was hot and moist, and she felt as if Tate had been holding it forever, not just a moment. Her heart was beating so hard that the blood pounding in her ears effectively drowned out any other sound. The words "Tate Monroe" echoed in her head.

CHAPTER SEVEN

Tate furiously pounded on the Down button for the elevator. *Victoria Sosa? Who the fuck is Victoria Sosa?* When the doors closed behind her she pulled out her cell phone and dialed the familiar number. She hung up when the elevator stopped at another floor and several people got in. Her call would have to wait until she had more privacy.

When the last person exited she repeated the actions with her phone and strode through the lobby. Someone answered her call as she exited, and she didn't waste any time with pleasant formalities.

"Who the fuck is Victoria Sosa?" she bellowed into the phone. She kept walking, not wanting to have the Sosa woman come up behind her and overhear her conversation. That was what she would have done if the roles were reversed. *All's fair in love, war, and business, and all that crap.* The people she passed could hear only her side of the conversation, and she didn't care if they thought she was being rude.

"You heard me. Some woman named Victoria Sosa seems to have made an offer for Braxton too. I am now in a bidding war and I'm not happy." Tate shouted the last few words.

"How am I supposed to know? That's what I pay you for, and right now I'm about ready to yank your chain so hard you'll see your toes when you close your eyes at night." Tate had to stop at the corner for a red light. She glanced around to make sure she didn't recognize anyone, especially Victoria Sosa.

"I'm headed back to my office. You have thirty minutes to be standing in front of me with her social security number, the name of her best friend in high school, and how many times a week she has sex. Do I make myself clear?" The woman beside Tate glanced at her and stifled a laugh. Tate hung up and said, "You just can't get good help anymore," as she stepped off the curb.

Exactly thirty-two minutes later Max McDonald was not standing, but quivering in front of Tate's desk. She had not indicated he was welcome to sit down, because he wasn't. She was furious that she had gone into that meeting not knowing everything possible about Braxton. She could have made a fool of herself—worse yet, completely lost the deal. She was relieved that she hadn't said anything damaging to Victoria while they were waiting for Braxton. And what in the hell was he up to? McDonald squirmed in front of her and she wanted him out of her office. She detested incompetence, and this lapse was unforgivable. But he had what she needed.

"Don't stand there like an idiot. I'm waiting for the information I *should* have had a week ago." She drummed her fingers on the top of her desk.

"Victoria Crystal Sosa, born May 23, 1965. Parents Lawrence and—"

"All that will be in your report. Get to the important part."

"She is the CEO of Drake Pharmaceuticals, a twelve-billion-dollar firm based here in Atlanta. She's been at the helm eight years, and my sources say she is extremely well liked and an effective leader. They also tell me they need Braxton to shore up their operations or they'll go under. Sosa is getting some serious heat from her board to clinch Braxton, and her ass is on the street if she doesn't. They don't have much to offer in the way of cash, so they'll probably propose some sort of joint partnership or a similar deal."

Tate mercifully tossed McDonald out of her office ten minutes later after she heard his complete report. Her mind was spinning because of the quick shift of events, but as she processed the information the familiar tingling sensation she always experienced at the prospect of a challenging duel began. She hadn't been this excited about a deal in a long time. Lately each one had just been more of the same—no thrilling chase, no maneuvering, and little of the one-upmanship that came with a takeover. She easily negotiated, compromised, and more often than not bullied the other company into seeing things her way. The process had gone stale without her even being aware of it.

Lifting her feet onto her desk, Tate leaned back in her chair and steepled her fingers under her chin. She sat that way for several long minutes, weighing everything McDonald had told her about Victoria against her own impressions of the woman.

Tate hadn't paid much attention to her when she ran into her in Braxton's lobby, dismissing her as a fortysomething straight woman with kids, a minivan, and a husband whose belly hung over his belt buckle. What she saw this morning was anything but. She might have a kid and drive a boring car, but Victoria Sosa was anything but straight.

Victoria's hair had been pulled back and secured at the back of her neck with something Tate couldn't see, but the style highlighted her high, strong cheekbones. Her perfectly shaped eyebrows arched above vivid blue eyes the color of the water in Cancun. When they shook hands Tate felt the familiar tug of sexual attraction, and if they had been in different surroundings she might have done something about it. Tate had immediately missed the contact when Victoria released her hand, but had been too focused on herself and what she didn't know about Victoria to really be aware of her reaction until now.

She sat there for the next hour searching the Internet for any additional information on Victoria Sosa. There was plenty, Google showing 8,459 hits. Most were of her college career at UCLA, detailing her years on the volleyball team, three of which she was a starter, and finally her final game when she won a gold medal at the 1984 Olympics. The remainder of the information concerned mainly her professional rise through the ranks of several biomedical firms and her ultimate selection as CEO of Drake.

Admitting that she was impressed, Tate pushed away from her computer. She had to brief Clayton on the new development, and he would probably give her more shit about how important it was to her career to bring in Braxton. She wasn't concerned. She was already formulating a game plan that included the suddenly very attractive Victoria Sosa.

❖

"Who in the hell is Tate Monroe?" Victoria had immediately called Albert and told him to have her staff in her office when she got back. Albert must have told them she was angry because not one of her trusted advisors said anything as she glared at each of them, fighting to control her anger.

"No one in this room knows who she is? No one has their ear to the street to know that she's made an offer to Braxton?" She looked each one in the eye before she moved on to the next. "No one knows why I walked into a meeting with Peter Braxton fully confident that he would agree to our proposal and ended up almost being put in my place by a thirty-year-old hotshot who was just as shocked as I was?" Her voice was rising in pitch and she took a few deep, calming breaths. Still no one said anything.

"That's exactly how I felt." She was calmer now than when she first sat down, though her hands were still shaking from the scene in Braxton's conference room. More than once on the drive back to her office she almost rear-ended the car in front of her. She had pulled into the parking garage on automatic pilot and didn't remember riding the elevator to her floor.

"Now, I am rarely a bitch and I try hard not to lose my temper, but I am not winning that battle today."

Her friend Claire was the first to speak. "I'm sorry, Victoria."

Several heads nodded in agreement.

"You're sorry about what? That you didn't do your jobs and I was left hanging with my butt in my hands? Drake needs this deal. I thought you all understood that fact. We cannot afford to screw this up, and let me tell you something, ladies and gentlemen. Your incompetence almost did us in. I take complete responsibility for this breakdown, but I rely on you to tell me things I have no way of knowing, and when I...no, when Drake," Victoria corrected herself, "when Drake needed you the most, you didn't come through. We very well could lose this deal." She didn't need to tell everyone what that meant. Thousands of people would be out of a job, with no paycheck or healthcare coverage.

Victoria didn't say anything else. One by one her staff left the room. Claire stayed behind.

"What is it, Claire?"

"Don't you think you were a bit hard on them?"

Claire was probably the closest she had to a best friend, but right now she was her CFO and Victoria had no trouble separating the two. "No, I don't. I don't have any idea when Monroe made her offer to Braxton, but I should have known there was at least the possibility of multiple offers for Braxton on the table even before I approached him the first time. I definitely should have had the information before this morning."

"Victoria, you've been under a lot of stress lately," Claire said.

Victoria wanted to laugh but didn't dare. She was afraid she might cry instead. In the past month she had averaged three or four hours of sleep a night, and with the frequent headaches she was experiencing, her blood pressure must be elevated to dangerous levels. She had vowed several times last week to try to get to the gym, but the operative word was *try*.

"That has nothing to do with it, Claire, and you know it. You of all people understand how much this company means to me, and I thought it meant the same to everyone else too."

"That's not fair, Victoria."

"Isn't it? Then how could this have happened?"

Claire didn't answer.

"I admit the proposal I presented to Braxton was the best thing for both of us, but because it was such a no-brainer, did that make us complacent on anything else? All I know is I was almost handed my head in my hands this morning by someone young enough to put us all to shame. We have nothing left to offer Braxton, and now we're in a bidding war."

Only in the presence of her friend would she drop her head in her hands like she did now. *What am I going to do?*

CHAPTER EIGHT

Victoria gathered her briefcase and suit jacket as the voice from the speaker called her flight. True to Braxton's word, his assistant Susan had worked with Albert to rearrange her schedule, and the week after Labor Day she was on the four-thirty flight from Atlanta to Chicago. The seats in first class were occupied except the one designated as 2C, and after she put her briefcase in the overhead compartment she slid into its soft leather. She buckled her seat belt, then sipped a glass of sparkling water that the flight attendant promptly offered her.

The man beside her was engrossed in his *Wall Street Journal*, and Victoria appreciated the fact that he wasn't interested in chit-chat. She had been on flights where her neighbor obviously wanted to become best friends, whether the flight lasted one hour or fifteen.

She was tired. She had gone out to dinner with Carole last night and told her about the condition Braxton had put on their bid for his company. Carole was as surprised as Victoria and commented several times how odd the requirement was. While Victoria described Tate, it was as if she was sitting across the table from her. She recalled her vivid green eyes and the no-bullshit way she looked at both her and Braxton. Victoria laughed when she compared Tate's walk to a jungle cat's. She was probably on the prowl in her personal life too.

When Carole suggested they return to her place Victoria begged off, citing her flight today, but lately she was increasingly less interested in sex. They rarely slept over when they met for dinner and ended the evening with sex. Each of them preferred to sleep in her own bed, or at least one or the other had an early meeting the next day. Lately their dates seemed more like a reoccurring obligation on Victoria's calendar than an occasion she looked forward to.

Opening the folder Albert handed her on her way out the door, she settled in to reread the complete dossier on Tate Monroe. She had read it several times already, as was her practice with all important documents, but each time she did she retrieved another tidbit of information or impression of her adversary. She had been impressed that Tate had gone to Wharton but was not impressed with her choice of employment.

Her boss, Clayton Sumner, was well known for his greed. He was supposedly the person that Gordon Gekko was modeled after in the movie *Wall Street*. Sumner probably had the trademark on the most famous line in the film, "Greed is good," and received royalties every day. His firm ran over companies like they were toy soldiers, crushing and dismantling everything in its path and leaving nothing but a huge pile of money for himself. Thousands of people had directly lost their jobs due to him. And when suppliers and customers of the companies he shut down also had to close, his greed affected hundreds of thousands more people downstream.

Victoria read the piece of paper that detailed Tate's personal life. She was definitely a lesbian and unashamed of her lifestyle. She didn't appear to have a steady relationship, but the accompanying photos showed a different woman on her arm every time she appeared in public. A minor note about her parents briefly stated that her father lived in a mobile-home park in Alabama. No other relatives were mentioned. As a matter of fact, neither was anything else. Tate seemed to have a sparse personal life.

Studying the five-by-seven glossy photo of Tate, Victoria felt old. Tate's skin was firm, with only a few small lines around her eyes, unlike the multiple deep ones Victoria had noticed on her face this morning in the bathroom mirror. Where did they all suddenly come from? It wasn't as if they were there last week. Were they? And Tate's eyes. She was gazing directly into the camera, and Victoria had to remember she was viewing a picture, not the real thing.

Victoria had seen those eyes look just the way they did now, very dark and twinkling with amusement. She studied the picture more intently. Was it her imagination or was something hiding deep inside the pools of green?

❖

Tate couldn't wait to get off the plane when it touched down shortly after eight. She had been traveling for a week, and this was her sixth flight in as many days. If she had to take her shoes off and her laptop out of her briefcase one more time, she'd scream.

It had been so much fun when she had first started flying on business. Each trip was exciting and she felt important. She had never flown as a child, her parents too worthless to hold a job or go anywhere other than the local bar and the quick mart for cigarettes. Joey Monroe couldn't keep a dime in his pocket or a commitment. He played poker with his buddies every Friday night, and between the beer and his bad luck he usually lost more than he won, leaving his family to scramble for just about everything. Tate went to bed hungry most of her childhood.

She was the subject of snickers and pointing fingers when she went into the grocery store for her mother, who was typically too bruised or drunk to leave the house. She felt the clerk's sympathy when she didn't have enough money to pay for what they needed to get through a few more days. Often they charged her for only half of what she put on the checkout counter. She didn't want their pity, but pride didn't fill her empty stomach.

The only thing she remembered about her father's job was that he was always bitching about it. Her friends had fathers who worked, and they took vacations to Disneyland or the beach or just to visit relatives. The farthest Tate got out of town was when she ran off with Camille Masterson in high school.

Tate was a sophomore when Camille, a senior, first came on to her. Camille, her first real girlfriend, had much more experience in the sex department than Tate, who had just "fiddled around," as she called it, with one or two girls at a slumber party. Camille had a car and a fake ID, and Tate was totally smitten. One night after the football game Camille suggested they drive to the next town and get beer. Tate tried hard to act as mature and sophisticated as Camille, but when she threw up all over the inside of her Chevy, she knew she would never see Camille again.

It wasn't until she was a junior in high school that she thought she would ever have an office, let alone the one she was sitting in now. Her high school guidance counselor had encouraged her to take the SAT, the massive college entrance test that could be her ticket to higher education. The exam consisted of ten sections, each of which had to be completed within a certain amount of time. Tate finished section after section before anyone else, and when she put her pencil down for the last time, four minutes remained. She double-checked her answers and when the proctor signaled time was up, she was a nervous wreck. By the time they were dismissed, her knees were shaking so bad she thought she might fall as she practically ran out the door.

A scholarship to Ohio State took her away from Hillsdale and she never looked back. Her mother died of pneumonia the summer she graduated from high school, and no one was there to see Tate off when she boarded the Greyhound bus bound for Columbus.

Now traveling, even with the comfort and amenities of first class, was just a pain in the ass, she thought, working her way through the congested walkway at O'Hare. She chuckled because she always thought that flying into Chicago was exactly like the childhood story called "The Tortoise and the Hare." You flew six hundred miles an hour to get there, then moved like a snail once you did.

Thankful she didn't have to check any luggage, Tate flagged down a cab and gave the driver the name of her hotel. She had been to Chicago several times for business and smiled to herself, remembering how on more than one occasion she was able to combine business with pleasure.

When she had thought about pleasure the past few days, the face of Victoria Sosa always came to mind. Even last night when the lovely waitress from the restaurant was writhing under her, Victoria intruded on her thoughts. Tate rarely fantasized about one woman when she was making love to another, but what the hell? They were total strangers both getting what they wanted, and Tate didn't hear the woman complain. As a matter of fact she—

"Hey lady, we're here," the cabbie said.

Tate glanced around, noticing the familiar landmarks, and tossed the driver a fifty-dollar bill. "Keep the change," she said, grabbing her overnight bag and briefcase. The bellman immediately took both items as she stepped out of the cab and into the lobby. They would miraculously appear in her room in about fifteen minutes, and she dismissed them as she walked to the registration desk.

❖

Victoria wandered down Wacker Drive searching for a quiet restaurant. She needed to review her notes for tomorrow's meeting with Braxton, and even though she had read about the operations they would be touring tomorrow a dozen times, she wanted to re-familiarize herself with them. Several couples were emerging from a doorway about fifteen feet ahead of her, and she glanced into the adjacent window. The interior was dimly lit, but not so dark that she wouldn't be able to see to read or make notes.

She grabbed the door before it closed behind the last couple and stepped inside. Several tables were open, so she didn't have to wait long to be seated.

She had just taken a sip of her wine when she glanced at the door. Standing just inside and looking right at her was Tate Monroe, dressed in khaki trousers and a light green polo shirt. Victoria's stomach contracted and she looked away before propriety necessitated she invite Tate to join her. She wouldn't accept anyway; they were rivals, after all. Better yet…she thought, catching Tate's eye and motioning her over.

Tate carried herself with an ease that said she was comfortable with herself in any surroundings. She obviously knew her smoldering sensuality made more than a few heads in any room turn. Victoria almost choked when she actually thought about Tate sexually. She never had fantasies like this during business dealings. In fact, she never had thoughts like this when she wasn't working. Something was definitely wrong with that scenario, she realized.

"Would you like to join me?" Victoria asked Tate, who seemed as surprised at the invitation as she herself was.

"Better the enemy you know?"

"Something like that," Victoria replied, a little breathless. She moved her folder off the chair next to her and tapped on the seat, indicating for Tate to sit down.

The waiter appeared out of nowhere and took Tate's drink order. When he left, Tate concentrated her full attention on her and Victoria felt the effect. The sounds of the restaurant diminished, the lighting became sharper, her senses more focused. The feeling shocked her, and she took another sip of her drink to give herself a minute to regain control.

Tate asked after her drink arrived, "What would your boss say if he saw us sitting together?"

"That I was learning more about the competition." Victoria tossed the question back at her. "How about yours?"

"Who was that beautiful woman you were having a drink with?" Tate replied smoothly.

Victoria touched her fork, a nervous gesture. "Really?" she asked skeptically.

"Actually, he'd say something crude, but the gist would be the same. And you are a beautiful woman."

The way Tate said *beautiful woman* made Victoria feel every bit a woman. She hadn't thought of herself as feminine lately, or even female. She was all about work, work, work, without a minute to herself in weeks. She liked to pamper herself on Sundays by visiting the spa for a full-body massage, facial, and manicure. It had been months since she'd seen the inside of the salon. She didn't need the pretense of perfect hair and makeup, but lately even the sexy lingerie she wore under her business suits wasn't doing the trick. The woman in her was flattered, the businesswoman slightly annoyed that Tate was hitting on her.

"Thank you," she managed to say without sounding too affected by the compliment. "I understand you work for Clayton Sumner." It was both a statement and a question. Victoria's heart tripped when Tate smiled and chuckled softly. It tripped again when Tate pinned her eyes.

"And I understand you work for Edward Hamacher," Tate countered. Tate held her gaze. "He's a first-class prick."

Victoria wasn't sure she heard Tate correctly. Had she just called the chairman of her board a prick? Her face must have given away her confusion.

"You heard me correctly, he's a prick. I went to college with his daughter, and if he's anything like he was as a father, he's, well…" Tate didn't need to finish her comment.

"Really?" Victoria was surprised at how easily Tate voiced her opinion on her business without regard to the potential consequences.

"Really. His daughter hated going home on the weekends. He would summon her, and she knew he would cut her off immediately if she disobeyed. He never hit her or anything like that, but he had control over her that made me sick."

"I'd rather not talk about Edward, if you don't mind. He is, after all, my boss." Victoria wanted to hear more but didn't trust this woman and certainly didn't want to give the impression she agreed with her. Even though she did.

"Fair enough. How do you know Braxton's wife?" She had obviously noticed his comment to Victoria at their first meeting.

"I played volleyball for UCLA. His wife, or actually his girlfriend at the time, played for Stanford. We beat them for the NCAA Championship."

"Ouch. I hope he doesn't hold that against you."

The waiter hovered, waiting to take their dinner order. Tate looked at Victoria hopefully. "Did your invitation include dinner or is this just a drive-by chat?"

Victoria weighed her options. She could eat alone for the umpteenth time this month or allow Tate to remain and get to know her better.

"If you're hungry, you're welcome."

"Okay. What are you having?" Tate easily changed the subject.

Victoria hadn't had a chance to look at the menu, but she had been craving pasta when she came in. Now she wasn't hungry for anything except Tate, whose charm and physical magnetism captivated her. The attraction between them was so strong Victoria would have to be on her toes not to let herself fall into it.

She focused on her menu, acutely aware of Tate looking at her over the top of hers. "I think I'll have the stuffed shells. You?" She lifted her eyes and kept her gaze steady.

"I feel decadent tonight." Tate hesitated and her eyes changed to a smoldering green. "I'm having the chicken Alfredo. Heart attack on a plate. I'm going to live on the edge."

Victoria had the impression that Tate more often than not lived a little dangerously. She seemed to embrace life unabashedly—took what she wanted and left nothing behind.

Victoria shuddered, then flexed her shoulders in a weak attempt to disguise her reaction.

"So, Victoria. May I call you Victoria?" Tate asked politely. Victoria nodded. "What do you do when you're not trying to buy companies?"

The bread had arrived and Victoria cut off a piece. "I run one," she replied, spreading butter over the warm bread.

"So I gather. Besides that? What do you do for fun?" Tate tore off a chunk of bread and popped it in her mouth all in one motion.

"Fun?" Victoria asked, feeling as if she had never heard the word before. Actually she had lost her train of thought when Tate's mouth opened and she spotted her tongue just before she closed it with the bread inside.

"Yes, you know fun? The things you do when you're not working?" Tate tore off another piece of bread and leaned back in her chair. "Please don't tell me all you do is work? All work and no play makes you a dull girl."

Victoria opened her mouth to say something caustic, but changed her mind when she saw amusement glinting in Tate's eyes. "I'm not a dull girl," she replied emphatically.

"Really?"

"Yes, really."

"Wanna skip all this pretense and just go back to my room?" Tate propositioned her as if it were the most natural thing in the world.

Pulse pounding in her ears and throbbing between her legs from Tate's blatant advance, Victoria was somehow able to reply. "And why would I want to do that?"

The waiter delivered their meal and Tate took a bite of her dinner. "Mmm," she moaned, then looked directly at Victoria. "Just like I wanted it. Sinfully delicious."

Victoria was speechless while Tate took another bite, then said, "Because we're attracted to each other and I think we could have some fun. I know I would."

Victoria went from mesmerized to stunned that Tate was actually proposing that they have sex. They were fighting for the same company. Why in God's name did she think Victoria would roll over, for lack of a better phrase, and jump into bed with her? Did she look desperate or lonely or simply stupid?

Wanting to slap the smug expression off Tate's face, Victoria stabbed her pasta instead. It would not be in her best interest to piss this woman off, however much she wanted to. She decided to play along instead, knowing she would never have sex with Tate.

"Pretty sure of yourself, aren't you?"

"No complaints that I've heard. Why? Have you heard something?" Tate pretended to be fearful of her response.

Tate *was* charming in a rogue kind of way, with her quick wit and the mischievous twinkle in her eyes. She was very attractive, her face free of flaws except a tiny mole on her jawline. Her neatly shaped eyebrows were raised in expectation of Victoria's answer to her question. "Do I look like the kind of woman who would kiss and tell?"

"That's another reason why we should hurry and have dessert in bed. Because you *won't* kiss and tell." Tate's eyes were smoldering, like embers reflected from the soft candlelight in the center of the table.

Victoria squeezed her legs together under the safety of the long tablecloth, which did little to assuage the throbbing that was distracting her from thinking clearly. But that only made the feeling worse. She resented the way her body was betraying her.

"As tempted as I am, I'll try to restrain myself." She was tempted; very tempted. Jeez, Victoria thought. Didn't I just say there was no way I'd have sex with her? God, this woman is a magnet.

Tate laid on the charm that Victoria imagined had won over more than a few hesitant women. "Ah, come on. Live a little."

Victoria reached down deep in her conscious self for control. "I'm quite happy with my life right now, thank you."

Tate pressed her leg against Victoria's. "You sure there's nothing I can do to change your mind?"

Oh, there's plenty you can do to change my mind, but I have too much to lose for a night of sex, even if it is with you. She forced an upbeat smile. "Nope, not a thing." She was certain Tate saw right through her.

CHAPTER NINE

The coffee was hot and Tate burned her tongue. *Shit! Another thing I didn't need.* Along with a sleepless night she'd stubbed her toe on the doorjamb on her way to the shower this morning—all because she couldn't stop thinking about Victoria. She had arrived at Braxton's regional headquarters early, hoping to have a few minutes alone with Victoria. She woke up this morning wanting to see her, and even though she was excited she was also troubled. She would do anything to learn more about Victoria's plans to acquire Braxton, including flirting and flattering her. Her first impression of Victoria had drastically changed, and Tate was surprised to find her intelligent and oddly attractive.

Their dinner had ended too soon, and when Victoria jumped into a cab after paying the bill, Tate felt alone. It was ridiculous. She was in one of the largest cities in the world. She went back into the restaurant but this time sat at the bar drinking until she got herself together enough to go back to her hotel room. It was as empty as she knew it would be, and when she did sleep she dreamed of Victoria.

Victoria entered the conference room, accompanied by at least eight other people. She was wearing tan slacks with a navy double-breasted blazer over a pale blue blouse, and the jacket brought out the color of her eyes. Her hair was gathered in the back like Tate had always seen it. Except for last night, she thought.

Last night Victoria's hair was down and Tate had fought the urge to run her fingers through it. It had looked like wheat blowing in a field and Tate swore she could smell the fresh scent wafting across the table. She had moved close to Victoria when she held the door of her cab. When she slid by her and into the cab, Tate inhaled the deep fragrance. She smelled it now from all the way across the room.

Everyone around the table introduced themselves, and after two hours of slides, charts, and graphs, Braxton stood and led them out of the room. Tate let Victoria go first, which gave her a prime view of her backside rather than Braxton's.

Victoria's clothes fit perfectly, accentuating her curves without calling attention to them. The alligator skin of her flat-heeled shoes gleamed under the bright lights. Today her hair was held together by a wide blue clip that Tate knew she could easily unfasten with one hand. Tate was so engrossed in watching the sway of her hips she almost ran into the back of one of Braxton's men when he stopped, but caught herself before she made contact.

Victoria was listening intently to the man who had introduced himself as the head of engineering. She stood up straight, which was unusual for a woman of her height. She hadn't slouched even a little when she shook hands with all the men this morning. Tate found it amusing that all of Braxton's staff members were men, and two women were vying for their company, one of them taller than everyone there. They probably had no clue that they both were lesbians. What were the odds?

Victoria swung her gaze at Tate, who gave her best yes-I-was-looking-at-you smile. She wasn't embarrassed to be caught. A woman should find it flattering when another woman wanted to look at her. Especially when Victoria's expression was so transparent. Victoria glanced away, but not before Tate saw an answering look in her eyes. Tate grinned and continued to keep her eyes glued to Victoria, but now she paid more attention to what the man in front of them was saying. Even if she got Victoria into bed, she still needed to get this deal.

❖

Victoria had just settled in the backseat of the taxi, exhausted after the endless tour of the facility. She heard a knock and saw Tate motioning for her to roll down the window. Against her better judgment she did. She had fought the urge to stare at Tate all afternoon, especially once she knew Tate was doing so. She felt, rather than saw, her eyes move all over her body, and it was particularly unnerving that Tate stayed behind her the entire day. The bottom of Victoria's jacket fell below her ass, but Tate was probably picturing it just the same. Victoria felt thoroughly ravished and Tate hadn't laid a finger on her.

"Hey, I thought we might grab some dinner. Strictly personal. We can talk about the weather, politics, or religion. That should keep the conversation lively."

Victoria was tired of battling the urge to fight her attraction to Tate, but she couldn't give in. There was too much at stake, and their tour of the facility today strengthened her belief.

"What, no discussion about sex?" Victoria's father had always told her that you should never discuss sex, politics, or religion because you would never get the other person to change their view. As soon as the word was out of her mouth she wanted to pull it back in. Tate's eyes lit up.

"I'd rather have it than talk about it, but if you insist."

Tate's smile transformed her face. Her perfectly straight teeth were white, and the dimple in her left cheek that Victoria hadn't noticed before made her look much younger. Like she needed any help in that area, Victoria thought.

"Hey, maybe we could combine the two. You know, kill two birds with one stone, multitask, or whatever you'd like to call it," Tate added.

"Inappropriate is what I'd call it." God, she hated sounding like a prude. "But thanks anyway. I'm on my way to the airport."

Tate looked as if she would try to cajole her but must have thought better of it. Instead she said, "Okay, but if you change your mind I'm at the Hilton on Michigan Avenue. Anytime is fine. I usually don't go to bed until late. Unless I have a reason to."

"Well, I won't be your reason."

Victoria told the cab driver to take her to O'Hare airport. *Good God, Victoria. You act as if you haven't had sex in years. Take your head out of your crotch and get with it. This is the biggest deal of your life and you're thinking about a woman. And a young one, at that.* Tate was more than ten years younger than she was, which was too much of an age difference at this stage of her life. She hit herself on the forehead. *Snap out of it. Stop thinking of her as a date, or a potential lover. She is not, cannot, and will not be any of those.* She repeated her statement to herself until she stepped out of the cab.

CHAPTER TEN

Victoria checked into her Phoenix hotel well after midnight. She could have taken a flight the following morning but always preferred to get to her destination as early as possible.

After a quick shower she logged on to her e-mail. As usual she had over a hundred messages in her in-box. Was there a technological devil that caused the messages to reproduce the longer they were unread? She sorted them by sender and read the ones from her staff first. Most were simply FYI or minor, but the note from Claire was cryptic and she frowned as she read it. Their major banker had made an appointment to meet with her and Claire late next week. As Victoria typed her reply she knew the banker wouldn't bring good news.

The pressure to ink the Braxton deal was enormous. In addition to their shareholders, thousands of people depended on Drake for their livelihood. The loss of revenue would impact the companies they purchased products and services from if they lost Drake as a customer, and the downstream effect, the loss of treatment options for their patients, was what kept her up at night. She could not fail. People would die, and she couldn't live with that fact on her conscience.

The alarm clock screamed at five fifteen, and Victoria rolled over, eyes grainy from lack of sleep, and cursed the time difference between Phoenix and New York. Three hours of sleep wasn't nearly enough, but she had a conference call with one of Drake's suppliers soon. It was another in a long line of calls containing assurances that Drake was solvent and would continue to pay their bills on time.

She crawled out of bed at the knock on her door. After verifying through the peephole that it was room service with the coffee she had pre-ordered, she unlatched the chain and swung open the door.

Ninety minutes later, dressed and sipping her fourth cup of coffee she followed the directions that the soft, melodic voice from the rental car's GPS system provided. The research arm of Braxton was located on a sixty-acre tract at the northern edge of the Phoenix city limits. If the calm voice hadn't told her to make a left in a hundred feet, she would have missed the subtle sign that indicated the road to the facility.

Saguaro cactus, paloverde trees, and creosote bushes surrounded the two-lane road carved out of the middle of the desert. As she drove she admired the beauty of the desolate terrain. Instead of dull and lifeless, it soothed and almost overwhelmed her. The power of nature to overcome drought and extreme heat made her feel insignificant.

Braxton was waiting for her in the cool lobby of the building. They chatted for a few minutes before Tate arrived and they received visitor badges, then let the buxom security guard check their briefcases for unauthorized cameras.

The routine was similar to their tour in Chicago, beginning with a briefing by the senior staff of the facility. Victoria met Tate's eyes as she sat in the vacant chair next to her.

"Here we go again," Tate said when the lights dimmed and the first slide of the presentation flickered to life on the large white screen.

Victoria couldn't help but smile because she felt exactly the same way. As much as she wanted, no, needed Braxton, she had a hard time focusing on the staff member's presentation. She had a perfect view of Tate and could look at her almost without being noticed. Her profile accentuated a strong jaw, and Victoria guessed that a break had caused the small bump on the bridge of her nose. She could picture Tate getting into a skirmish or even a brawl. More than likely someone had called her on her cocky attitude a time or two. Somehow Victoria suspected that, even with a broken nose, Tate had come out ahead.

She refocused on the presenter and decided to take notes to keep her eyes off Tate and her mind on what was being said. She had a knack for remembering details, however minor, and rarely needed to take notes. But for the first time in a long time she needed something to focus on.

The day finally ended and Victoria couldn't wait to get off her feet, having walked what seemed like miles on the hard tile floor of the huge facility. Even though she had worn flat, comfortable shoes her lower back ached and her left knee throbbed. She wanted nothing other than to soak in the Jacuzzi tub and drink a glass of wine. After spending the day with Tate constantly nearby, two or three glasses sounded even better. She disengaged the car's alarm and, over the beep, heard someone call her name.

Tate sauntered toward her on legs that went all the way to the ground, as her father used to say. During the instant Victoria pictured them wrapped around her, her stomach jumped. She took a few quick deep breaths before Tate stopped in front of her.

"At the risk of being rejected again, would you like to grab some dinner?"

After the introductory briefing, Tate had stayed by her shoulder all day. She murmured flippant comments under her breath, which, like her first of the morning, were exactly what Victoria was thinking. The unfamiliar fragrance of her cologne tickled Victoria's nose.

"You're persistent." Tate rewarded Victoria with one of her dazzling smiles, and Victoria's stomach jumped again.

"I don't accept 'no' very well. It's usually just a stall tactic. Kind of like playing hard to get."

"Is that how you see me? Playing hard to get?" Victoria asked before she thought about what she should say.

"Are you?" Tate cocked her head to the side.

"If I were, that would imply that I'm interested in you."

"Are you?" Tate repeated.

It was on the tip of her tongue to lie and say no, but instead she answered with a question herself. "Do you always hit on business associates?"

"Only the beautiful ones," Tate said simply.

With a woman like Tate, that answer was more than likely true. "Don't you find that difficult?"

"I have no trouble separating business and pleasure."

The way Tate said *pleasure* made a tingle trickle down Victoria's spine. Her voice was soft and warm and obviously very practiced. "Does the other side of the equation understand that separation?" A stab of jealousy pricked Victoria when she thought of another woman touching Tate.

Tate hesitated before she answered, giving Victoria the chance to draw her own conclusion. "My point exactly," she said, more confidently than she felt. She was drawn to Tate no matter how much she tried not to be. Something about Tate intrigued her as well as made her pulse race. She was young, charming, and smolderingly sensual. Victoria had no doubt that Tate would be more than able to cash the check her body was writing.

"You wouldn't make that mistake," Tate countered, shifting her weight from foot to foot as if trying to keep her balance during this verbal sparring match.

"How do you know?" Victoria was interested in Tate's answer since she herself didn't know if she could.

"Because you're a successful businesswoman. You understand business and what it takes to get what you want." Tate's eyes practically stroked her body, adding a different meaning to her statement.

Victoria's mouth went dry and she had trouble swallowing.

She wanted to reach for the car door handle but was afraid her shaking hand would betray her. Finally she dared to answer. "Yes, I do, and I've already told you that mixing the two isn't good for business. Whatever the circumstances or the understanding," she added. She wasn't sure which of the two of them she was trying to convince.

"Okay, I'll buy that. But we still have to eat. I promise I won't bite or try to seduce you over the entrée. I can't guarantee good behavior over dessert, though. It's my weakness and I often can't control myself."

Tate's smile and sparkling eyes made Victoria overrule her better judgment, and Tate followed her to a Phoenix restaurant that Braxton had recommended earlier in the day. The waiting area was crowded, and the waiting patrons grumbled as a hostess who couldn't take her eyes off Tate seated them. Their table against the window offered them a bird's-eye view of the city lights. In contrast, a lone candle flickered in the center of the white-cloth-covered table, creating an intimate atmosphere.

Tate scanned the wine list, congratulating herself for convincing Victoria to change her mind. Her confidence began to return. Women were all alike, she thought. They just needed a little persuasion to ease their guilt or take the decision out of their hands. However, she was slightly disappointed. She had expected more from Victoria.

"So what do you think?" Tate asked after the waiter took their drink order.

"About what?"

"Braxton."

"The man or the company?"

"Both." Tate didn't really expect Victoria to comment but she ventured down that path anyway. She had been trying to read him all day but he gave nothing away.

"Interesting," Victoria said.

"Which?"

"Both."

When Victoria didn't elaborate Tate decided not to press. She chose the personal route instead.

"So, Victoria, is anyone waiting at home for you to clinch this deal?" Tate loved the way Victoria's name sounded as it came from her lips. It was as elegant and sophisticated as the woman herself.

"I thought you were going to behave." Victoria sipped from the glass of wine the waiter had set in front of her.

"I am. I'm just making conversation."

"Uh-huh."

Tate faked being insulted. "What? I promised you wouldn't have to worry until dessert." She laughed and added, "What would you like to talk about?"

Victoria took another swallow of her wine, and Tate could practically feel the warm liquid slide down her long neck. She wanted to trace its path with her tongue. She was more attracted to Victoria than she could remember being to any other woman. The sensation slightly unnerved her, and she compensated by falling back on what she was most comfortable with—flirting.

"Baseball," Victoria answered, deadpan.

"Baseball?" Tate wasn't certain she heard her correctly through her haze of arousal.

"Yes, baseball. We're in the middle of the playoffs and every game matters. The Braves are a complete underdog to get to the Series, but I think they'll take it all." Victoria cut a chunk of bread from the bread basket. "You do follow baseball, don't you?"

"Not exactly." Tate was almost at a total loss. She wasn't exactly a fan. She enjoyed a game or two but had been so busy lately with the Braxton deal she had lost track of where they were in the season. Victoria laughed and Tate's heart jumped. She needed to repeat whatever she said if it caused Victoria's face to light up like it was now.

"You better be careful, Tate. You'll lose your lesbian

membership card if anyone finds out you don't follow the game," Victoria teased.

If she thought she liked saying Victoria's name, she practically melted when the roles were reversed. Victoria had rarely called her by her first name and when she did, Tate's stomach tingled. What would happen if she said it in the heat of passion?

Their dinner arrived and Tate enjoyed watching Victoria eat because she wasn't embarrassed to enjoy the food in front of her. Tate was amazed when she finished her steak, baked potato, and vegetables on top of the salad and three slices of bread before the main meal had arrived. *Where did she put it all?*

They kept up a casual conversation, Tate daring an occasional flirtatious comment. Victoria tossed them right back at her with an ease that challenged Tate to go even farther. When the waiter arrived with the dessert tray she looked at Victoria expectantly.

"Up to you," she said, smiling. "Just remember, I've given you fair warning." Tate wasn't sure if the flicker she saw in Victoria's eyes was due to the candle flame or some other flame she was more familiar with. She hoped it was the latter. She started to say something to that effect but was cut off when Victoria ordered the apple cobbler.

A recognizable throb started low in Tate's belly. "I see you're a risk taker. I like that in a woman." She closed the gap between them. "I like a lot of things I see in you, and I'm sure I'll like what I can't see even better." Tate lowered her eyes and her palms itched to cup the breasts that were moving up and down with Victoria's now-rapid breathing.

"You don't waste any time, do you?"

The tremor in Victoria's voice made Tate's confidence in getting this woman into bed grow. "No. Not when I see something I want." *And I definitely want you.* Earlier she had told Victoria that she always separated business from pleasure, but with Victoria she wanted both. Even though she was immensely attracted to her, her number-one goal was Clayton's job. One would get her the other, and she wouldn't let either opportunity get away. Nothing ever did and she wasn't about to start now.

"I guess I'll have to be on full alert then, won't I?" Victoria replied.

Tate noticed two things about Victoria that had changed in the last few minute. Her hand shook ever so slightly when she lifted her coffee cup to her lips, and her nipples were erect and hard under her blouse. Tate's confidence soared.

"Speaking of full alert," she said, not even trying to hide her stare at Victoria's nipples. "Is that—"

"You're not going there, Tate," Victoria said sternly.

"Uh-huh," she replied with no conviction.

"I mean it, Tate. You can look all you want because that's as far as you're getting."

"Tonight," Tate replied, and locked onto a pair of surprised blue eyes when she looked up.

❖

Victoria ordered a large pot of coffee from room service the next morning. She needed it. She had slept the entire night, but her dreams were filled with images of having sex with Tate.

She had never figured out exactly where they were, but they had enough privacy to make love in several places and in many different ways. First Tate pinned her to a wall and shoved her hand inside her pants, her lips moving rapidly down Victoria's neck. Her shirt was unbuttoned and the front of her bra was open. Tate alternately sucked and nipped her neck and breasts, driving her crazy. Victoria could actually feel the jolt of excitement shoot from her nipple to her clit when Tate bit it. She was helpless to do anything but wrap her arms around Tate's neck and hang on as one hand explored her warm center, the other wrapped around her waist.

Tate rubbed her clit faster and faster, each time driving her closer to orgasm. Victoria begged for release, and when it came it radiated from her toes to the tip of her head. She thought she would explode from the inside out, and as she cried Tate's name she dissolved into pleasure.

Victoria woke up after that one, her hand between her legs, the other pinching her nipple. She was embarrassed but not too much to finish what her dream had started. She fell back asleep immediately and drifted off to another erotic encounter with Tate.

This time she was the aggressor, and they were in the conference room adjacent to her office. The lights were on, the video projector displaying a chart with arrows going up and to the right. Business must be good, she thought, glancing at the screen.

Tate was sitting on the edge of the mahogany table, her legs spread, Victoria kneeling in front of her. Her shirt was open and she wore no bra. Tanned skin filled the open space, with just a hint of cleavage supplementing her androgynous look, but Tate was definitely all woman.

Victoria had read that you were not supposed to be able to smell in dreams, but that was definitely an old wives' tale. Tate had a freshness that Victoria had never encountered, and it pulled her closer. Drops of arousal glistened on swollen lips, dark curly hair, and the tip of her clitoris. Victoria wanted to stay in this spot forever and bask in the beauty of Tate, but she wanted to explore her even more.

Slowly she moved closer, each moment disappearing like sand in an hourglass. Tate had long since stopped sitting motionless, her hips thrusting forward eagerly as if trying to make contact with Victoria's mouth. Victoria held her breath as she snaked her tongue out for her first tentative taste of Tate's flesh. She was warm and wet and uttered Victoria's name softly. Tate's flesh quivered under Victoria's tongue, and her passion and desire threatened to overtake her. Forcing her own needs from her mind, she concentrated on giving Tate more pleasure than she had ever imagined possible. Slowly she explored every inch of her, alternating long languid licks with quick flicks of her tongue.

Tate leaned back, her arms no longer able to support her. She was moving so much Victoria wrapped her arms around her hips to hold her tight. Tate circled her back with her legs as if she were afraid Victoria would move away. No such thought entered Victoria's mind, and she memorized every sight, sound, and taste of Tate. Tate's breathing quickened, matching the thrust of her hips. Her clit hardened under Victoria's tongue and she slid first one then two fingers into Tate, whose muscles grasped her fingers tightly as she exploded in Victoria's mouth. Pulse after pulse of desire flowed out of her, her tight inner walls spasming around Victoria's fingers. Papers scattered across the table as Tate spread her arms and arched forward, gripping Victoria's hair and pulling her even closer. Victoria released her own desire as Tate held her tight, trembling under her mouth.

When the alarm clock shocked Victoria out of that dream she was totally confused as to where she was. She was breathing heavily, the room was unfamiliar, and she was soaked in sweat. It took her a minute to silence the beep blasting from the top of the nightstand, and she fell back onto the bed gasping. Her hands were shaking and her head spun when she had tried to sit up. She stumbled into the shower on shaking legs.

Her hands were still shaking when she pulled into the parking lot. She chose the same space she had occupied yesterday when Tate asked her to dinner. Maybe she should have taken her up on her offer to have sex. It wasn't as if she hadn't anyway, at least in her dreams. She gathered her briefcase, her wits, and her fortitude to face Tate this morning and walked on unsteady legs to the front door.

Their day was similar to the one before, except this time Victoria maneuvered herself behind Tate most of the time. Every time she looked at Tate, images of her sprawled on her conference table or her hand in her pants flashed in her mind. Her stomach was in knots, alternating between butterflies and throwing up. Finally after lunch the latter won and she was just able to escape to the ladies' room in time to heave the meal into the toilet. She was alone in the restroom, thankful that Tate hadn't followed her.

Fighting another wave of nausea, she leaned over the sink and splashed water on her face. She let it drip off her chin as her hands came back into focus. This was more than nerves over a woman. She had either eaten something that didn't agree with her or caught a bug. God, the last thing she needed was to come down with the flu. Lifting her head, Victoria studied her reflection in the mirror. She was pale and her hair suddenly looked as limp and lifeless as she felt. Pulling herself together and saying a silent prayer that she would get through the rest of the day, she opened the heavy door. Her legs were unsteady as she joined everyone waiting for the elevator. When the doors opened she was the last to step inside.

❖

Tate stood behind Victoria in the elevator and rubbed the back of her neck to ease the tension that had settled there. Braxton was to her left, glancing at his watch. Looking at Victoria's reflection in the mirrored doors, Tate thought she looked pale and tired. It had been a long day.

Tate smiled warmly into the mirror and Victoria's face grew paler. The tension in the small elevator grew and Victoria shifted her weight from foot to foot as if getting ready to bolt. When the doors finally opened, Victoria was the first one out, barely saying good-bye to Braxton, and hurried to her car, shutting the door as if it were a sanctuary.

What was going on? Tate didn't know Victoria, but she had been acting strangely all day and Tate was worried. She retraced the steps she had taken last night to Victoria's car.

"Is everything all right, Victoria? You've looked a little peaked all day."

"No, everything is fine," Victoria replied a little too quickly. Tate didn't believe her and bent down to see her better.

Victoria felt Tate's breath on her cheek as she leaned into the open window. Tate smelled like the cinnamon gum she was always chewing. It was a pleasant scent but not this time. Victoria's stomach lurched again. She hoped she didn't barf all over Tate's shoes.

"I don't believe you. You've been flushed all day and made more trips to the bathroom than anyone. Those guys were clueless but I know what's going on."

"Tate, I'm fine, really." She tried to sound convincing but her mind was losing the battle over her stomach.

"Bullshit. Move over."

Victoria was so surprised when Tate opened her door and motioned her to the passenger seat that she complied. She slid over, hesitantly grateful as Tate shifted the car into reverse and backed out of the space.

"Buckle your seat belt," Tate commanded. "Where are you staying?"

"I *was* at the Hyatt. I've already checked out," Victoria managed to say. Her flight was at nine that evening and she had planned to go straight from Braxton's to the airport. She flopped her head back on the headrest and closed her eyes, fighting the dizziness that threatened to overtake her.

"Victoria?" Tate's strong voice echoed in her head. "Victoria?"

"What?" she finally answered.

"We're here." Tate had taken her briefcase out of the backseat where she had tossed it.

"Where are we?"

"My hotel. I don't check out until tomorrow. Come on." Tate took her arm.

"Tate, I'm fine."

"Shut up" was all Tate said as she pulled her into the elevator. She pushed the number eight button and the glass-enclosed car shot upward so fast Victoria's ears popped.

Tate's jaw was clenched as she led Victoria down the plush hall, then stopped in front of the door bearing a polished brass plate that read 811. Tate slid her keycard into the slot and the electronic lock clicked once and the green light appeared. She opened the door and Victoria wished it were her room where she could step inside, crawl under the covers, and put this awful day behind her. But it was Tate's room and she was impatiently waiting for her to enter.

Tate closed the solid door behind her and Victoria looked around. The suite had two chairs, a love seat, and a small coffee table near the window. A modest desk complete with an open laptop, printer, fax machine, and comfortable-looking chair was nestled in the corner. Through open French doors Victoria could see the edge of a bed covered in a deep red comforter.

"The bathroom is through there. You look like hell. I'm not letting you leave until I know you're okay. Now go in the bathroom and splash some cold water on your face. It'll probably make you feel better."

Victoria did as she was told and pressed a wet washcloth to the back of her neck. She washed her face, brushed her teeth with her finger and Tate's toothpaste, and combed her hair. Shakily she opened the door.

Tate was sitting in the chair by the desk looking worried and intense.

"I feel better. I really need to go. I have to catch my flight tonight." Victoria had to leave, and in order to do that she had to convince Tate she was okay. "Really, I'm fine now. I must have eaten something that didn't agree with me."

"There are other flights and you're not going anywhere."

Victoria looked at Tate, feeling as if she had just asked her to strip and run around Wrigley Field. "Tate," she said, as the room began to swim.

Tate caught Victoria before she fell to the floor.

❖

The pounding in her head would not go away and Victoria felt as if she were in a thick fog trying to swim out. Her toes and fingers moved, but anything more strenuous made stars sparkle behind her eyes.

"Here, drink this," a soft voice said. A hand behind her neck helped her raise her head. She was so weak she could barely swallow.

"Come on, drink a little more. You're dehydrated and we've got to get some fluids in you. You'll feel better when you do."

The cool liquid soothed her parched throat, and she forced herself to take several more swallows.

"Okay, that's enough for now. We don't want it coming right back up."

Victoria fell back against the soft pillows and slept before waking again, this time more coherent than the last. She blinked several times, trying to focus. She must be dreaming, she thought. Tate was sitting in a chair beside her reading a book that Victoria recognized as the same one she had on her night table at home. *Where am I? What happened?* Tate must have sensed her stirring because she lowered the book and smiled.

"Hey, there. How are you feeling?"

Tate laid her palm on her forehead and then cupped her cheek. She had a worried expression. Victoria tried to respond but her tongue stuck to the roof of her mouth.

"Here, drink this. Can you sit up a little?"

Victoria tried, and a pair of strong arms immediately steadied and supported her.

"Take it easy. You've been out quite a while."

Tate stuffed a pillow behind her and sat on the side of the

bed. She handed her the glass and Victoria was grateful for the straw. This time she was able to voice her questions.

"What happened?"

"You fainted. You had food poisoning. At least that's what the doctor thinks."

"Doctor?"

"Yeah, you were pretty sick. When you didn't come to I called the front desk and they phoned a doctor. He said you should be okay in a day or two, once it's all out of your system."

Tate's words hit her like a blow to her achy stomach. *Oh, my God, I threw up in front of this woman.*

Tate smiled and encouraged her to drink some more. "Don't worry. You're not the first woman I've helped to the bathroom. Or the shower," she added when Victoria glanced down at her lack of clothing. "Sorry, I thought it was for the best. I was running out of T-shirts to put on you. I saved one for when you were through it all."

Victoria dropped her face in her hands and moaned. God, that made her head hurt.

"Don't be embarrassed. It's just your body's way of getting all the bad stuff out."

"Yeah, but you're not me."

"I have been," Tate replied calmly.

"You've puked and probably released other bodily things that I don't even want to think about in front of the CEO of the company you're trying to beat out for a deal? Please share that experience with me so I won't feel humiliated alone."

"Okay, maybe not exactly this situation. But I have been sick before and I appreciated someone taking care of me."

"You could have left me." Victoria sipped more Gatorade.

"I could have, but even though you may think I'm a callous bitch, I couldn't just leave you. You were really sick."

"Your mother would be proud," Victoria stated seriously. A cloud passed over Tate's face before it disappeared again.

"Actually my mother would have dumped you right inside

the door, taken your wallet, displayed the Do Not Disturb sign, and left. Good for you I read somewhere those aren't the best manners."

Victoria thought about what Tate had just said. Was it true or was she just making conversation?

"No, really, she would have, and she would have tried to sell me your BlackBerry." Tate nodded, emphasizing her point.

Victoria's head hurt too much to say anything other than "Thanks."

"Anytime." Tate stood and walked to the phone. "Do you feel up to eating something?"

"Maybe. What time is it?" Victoria looked around the room.

Tate turned the clock on the nightstand around to see the time. "Seven thirty."

"At night?" Victoria asked.

"Yep, like I said, you were pretty sick."

Victoria started to push the covers away but stopped when she realized she was totally naked. She felt her face flush. "Where are my clothes? I have to go." She surveyed the area for the clothes.

"Hanging in the closet but you're not going anywhere. The doctor said you need to rest and rehydrate, and that's exactly what you're going to do."

"I have to get to Brussels." Victoria spoke with very little determination.

"Yeah, well, so do I. You missed your flight, thank goodness. Can you imagine what would have happened if this hit when you were halfway across the ocean?"

Victoria looked around the room. She had to get out of here. She couldn't stay, and she certainly couldn't stay naked in front of Tate. Before she had a chance to think of anything else to say, Tate interrupted her thoughts.

"I found your itinerary in your briefcase. I changed your reservation to tomorrow evening."

My briefcase? What else did she see?

"I didn't snoop, if that's what you're thinking. I wanted to, but I didn't. I thought of calling your office, but today is Saturday so there's really no point. Your BlackBerry is locked so I couldn't call anyone else." Tate started to reach for the device. "Is there someone you should call?"

Victoria thought of Carole, but just as quickly dispelled the idea. Even though they had dinner the night before she left for Chicago, they hadn't really connected in several weeks, each tacitly admitting that nothing held them together.

"No, no one."

Tate appeared surprised, and Victoria wondered what she was thinking. That she was a loser, an orphan, an antisocial workaholic? And why all of a sudden did it matter what she thought?

"Okay, I'll call room service and have them send you some soup. It'll keep until you're ready. Do you feel up to a shower?"

Victoria did feel sticky and clammy, and she probably smelled awful. "I could probably use one." She looked around for something to put on.

Tate held up a robe. "Here. Let me help you. You're probably a little weak."

She was more weak than embarrassed by her nakedness. If what Tate said was true, she had already seen much more of her body than she wanted her to.

"Thanks," she replied, and slipped into the soft robe. Tate's arm around her gave her the support she needed until she felt more stable.

"I'll start the water and help you in. The maid left a shower seat you can sit on once you're inside. It'll give you some privacy."

Victoria was touched by Tate's kindness. She had never been this humiliated. How could she ever look Tate in the eye across the conference room table? She had wiped her face and probably her ass for the past twenty-four hours. How much worse could it get?

Victoria groaned from the relief the hot water provided as well as her embarrassment. She sat unmoving for several minutes, letting the streaming water slide over her aching body. Her stomach still had the cramps she vaguely remembered and her muscles were sore from heaving. Though her hands were steady when she reached for the shampoo, she had to gently massage her scalp so as not to inflame her headache.

"Everything okay in there?" Tate asked from the other side of the opaque curtain.

Victoria hoped she didn't peek inside to check on her, then chuckled at her shyness. "So far so good." Victoria could see Tate hesitate as if she were debating whether or not to believe her. "You were right, the water feels great."

"Okay. Take your time but don't overdo. Your soup should be here in a few minutes."

Tate started to leave the bathroom but Victoria stopped her. "Tate?"

"Yes?"

Victoria felt safe behind the flimsy curtain, but it gave her courage. "Thanks." She paused. "Thanks for everything." Victoria could hear the smile in Tate's voice when she replied.

"You're welcome."

Victoria didn't want Tate to leave the room. She had been leaning against the counter while Victoria was under the water, and her presence gave Victoria a sense of comfort that if she needed her again, she would be there for her. Who was this woman? She certainly wasn't what she had appeared to be up to this point. The snide comments, the cocky attitude, and the air of superiority had disappeared. In their place were kindness and consideration, and she was doing everything she could to help Victoria feel at ease.

Victoria shut off the water and Tate immediately handed her a towel.

"Thanks." Victoria dried off and wrapped the thick towel around her.

"Be careful standing up. The water was hot and you might be light-headed." Tate extended her hand to help Victoria out.

She was holding the robe Victoria had discarded earlier. Victoria slid her arms in and Tate reached around her to tie the sash in a knot. Victoria's stomach jumped. For a moment she thought she would be sick again, then realized that Tate's warm breath tickling her ear was the cause. Their eyes met in the mirror and Victoria saw something more than simple concern in Tate's. It flared for a moment before Tate broke contact and stepped away.

"Okay?" Tate asked, not reestablishing eye contact.

"Yeah, I'll just be a minute."

"Help yourself to whatever you need." Tate closed the door behind her.

❖

"For God's sake, Monroe, pull yourself together. The woman is sick, not to mention the fact that she could keep you from getting Clayton's job," Tate said under her breath as she paced around the room. "Stop remembering how soft her skin is or how firm her breasts are and how she looked lying in that bed."

At the time she'd been too concerned over Victoria's condition to pay any attention to the bare butt cheek that was exposed when the doctor gave her the shot. Tate's experience of ministering to the sick was limited to her date puking after too much alcohol. It surprised her that she felt the need to take care of Victoria. She wasn't any good when her friends were sick, even though she knew them.

"Did you say something?"

Victoria's voice coming from behind her startled her. How much had she heard? "Just talking to myself. Your soup is here," she added, changing the subject. She held the chair out for Victoria and sat beside her as she tasted the warm broth.

The spoon rattled in the empty bowl. The color had returned

to Victoria's face and her eyes weren't as glazed as before. She carried on a conversation between bites, and Tate was finally starting to believe that she was on the mend. The way Victoria looked had frightened her, almost to the point of panic. Usually she would gladly let her foe fall ill and swoop in to capture the prize, but she didn't feel that way with Victoria and didn't want to see her hurting. As Tate watched her, an unfamiliar warmth pulsed in her chest. Could this be nurturing, the desire to look after her, protect her from harm? If so, she had no idea why she felt this way. Victoria was the woman who stood between her and what she had dreamed of her entire life.

An only child, Tate grew up in the shadow of a worthless father and an uncaring mother, both of whom habitually told her she would never amount to anything. They said she was only good for having babies and that she needed to find a husband to take care of her before she got herself knocked up and saddled with a child like her mother had been. Her father often left his family to face the shame and embarrassment of his broken promises. She wouldn't let Victoria down when she needed her.

Her head hurt from thinking about her uncharacteristic behavior and the stress of the day, and she was tired. Victoria needed her rest as well. "You need to go back to bed. Don't argue," Tate said, when Victoria started to speak. "You're in no position to go anywhere other than right *there*." Tate pointed to the king-size bed.

"Where do you intend to sleep?"

"Same place." Tate nonchalantly pointed to the bed. Victoria's expression was an amalgamation of shock, fear, and fatigue. "I nursed you for two days. You don't expect me to sleep on the couch, do you?" Her tone was teasing but there was no real humor behind it.

"Since you put it that way. You *have* seen more of me and been more intimate with me than any woman I've been with in months, so there's no point in arguing. Change your clothes and let's get some sleep. You look like hell too." Victoria slid between the sheets, effectively ending the conversation.

Tate finished up in the bathroom and strode nervously into the bedroom. Victoria was nestled under the covers, the light on the nightstand casting a soft glow over the room. Any other time, if she had a woman in this position, she would have been on her without thinking twice. But this was Victoria in her bed, and she stopped when she reminded herself of that fact.

She wanted Victoria—wanted to explore her body in a non-medical way. She wanted to caress, not soothe. Have her sweat from desire, not fever, the whimpering sounds coming from her beautiful lips the result of pleasure, not pain. Tate had never wanted another woman like she wanted Victoria. Her power and grace were intoxicating, and Tate was almost overcome.

"What is it?" Victoria asked.

"Nothing." Tate continued to the bed. Pulling back the covers, she climbed onto the side opposite Victoria. "Everything okay?"

"Good for me. You?"

"I'm good. I left a light on in the front room in case you need to get some water or something from the minibar. Anything else you need, just ask. *Mi casa, a su casa*," she said in very poor Spanish, trying to assure Victoria that her "house" was Victoria's "house" as well.

Tate wanted to kiss Victoria but restrained herself. One kiss wouldn't be enough. She could probably persuade Victoria to make love, but she didn't want to have to convince her. She needed Victoria to want it as much as she did. Tate felt like a cad. The woman was still recovering from a serious illness and she was fantasizing about having sex with her.

CHAPTER ELEVEN

Victoria gathered her coat and scarf, made sure she had her room key, and closed the door behind her, too restless to stay in her room. She stopped at the concierge desk and asked for a local street map. She had never been to Brussels but knew that the city, like all cities in Europe, was filled with famous architecture, hundreds of shops to wander through, dozens of restaurants, and thousands of years of history. She had all day to explore, which would hopefully take her mind off Tate Monroe. They had flown here together, her seat next to Tate's in first class. Tate had insisted she sit next to her so she could keep an eye on her. Victoria had to admit she did feel more comfortable with Tate close by if she were to have a relapse.

She studied the map in the busy hotel lobby. It was only ten in the morning but guests were in various stages of checking out, waiting for taxis to take them to a meeting or, like her, holding a map, planning their day.

Victoria had checked in last night, and when she climbed between the cool, crisp sheets she had not slept well. Jet lag and the unfamiliarity of the hotel room caused some of her restlessness, but mostly she missed the warmth of Tate's body next to her. She had wakened several times during the night they shared a bed to find Tate curled behind her, an arm wrapped protectively around her. The soft, rhythmic breathing quickly lulled her back to sleep.

She woke up alone back in Phoenix, Tate in the shower and her suitcase unzipped and sitting on the couch. Tate must have retrieved it from the trunk of her rental car, and for the second time Victoria was touched by her thoughtfulness. After their flight to Brussels, they collected their bags and passed through customs, then separated, going to different hotels. Their meeting with Braxton was the following day.

Studying the map, she traced a route with her finger. She was headed for the Grand Place, the central town square in the heart of Brussels. Constructed in the early 1400s, it was the number-one tourist attraction in Belgium, and she couldn't wait to see it. Victoria folded the map and put it in her back pocket, comfortable that she knew the way. Brussels was a safe city, but she didn't want to advertise too loudly that she was a tourist. Of course as soon as she stepped out of a shop carrying a shopping bag, all pretense of being a local would vanish.

The streets were practically empty this early September morning. Europeans started their day far later than she was used to. Very few shops were open for business and she strolled in and out of those that were. She walked up and down the streets, often veering off her route, but not so far that she got lost. The streets were narrow, often with cars parked bumper to bumper, and she wondered how, with little to no room, they ever got out.

The closer she got to the Grand Place, the more the architecture began to change. Relatively modern buildings slowly transitioned into ones made of block and stone that reflected the era of the Grand Place. Small shops with narrow doorways were tucked into the buildings so discreet she almost missed them if she wasn't careful.

The chocolatiers were by far the most popular stores, followed closely by those that sold lace and, of course, the typical tourist trinkets. Mass-produced mugs, plates, and shot glasses bearing famous statues, buildings, and museums in Belgium were displayed in every store window. When she finally entered the Grand Place, she stopped and took it all in. It was more marvelous and stunning than she had imagined.

To her left was the Museum van de Stad Brussel Broodhuis. Directly across the street was the former Hotel de Ville, now the town hall. Next to it was the Maison des Brasseurs, a modest building, considering the size of the other buildings bordering the main square. Jostled by a fellow tourist, Victoria moved into the square.

There were more people here than she had seen on the street. A lone vendor was positioned in the center selling drawings of every famous building in Belgium. People posed for pictures or simply stood and gazed in awe. Young lovers walked hand in hand, families chatted, and an old woman holding on to the arm of a young man slowly walked across the expansive space.

Several restaurants bordered the square, and Victoria sat down at one of the tables on the patio. A waiter quickly appeared and she ordered a cappuccino. A movement out of the corner of her eye caught her attention, and she looked up at the same time Tate Monroe asked, "How are you feeling?"

Victoria didn't recognize Tate immediately. She hadn't expected to see anyone she knew, but the vivid green eyes couldn't belong to anyone but Tate. She looked young, her hair tousled by the wind, her cheeks flushed from the cold morning air. She was dressed in black, her leather jacket Victoria recognized as one she had almost bought from a J.Crew catalogue.

"Better, thanks to you."

"May I join you? I promise, no talk about your illness. And no talk about business," Tate added when Victoria didn't immediately answer.

"Would you like a cappuccino?" Victoria said without thinking and motioned for her to sit.

"Yes, I would, thank you." Tate settled onto the chair to her left.

Victoria flagged down the waiter and ordered.

"You speak French," Tate said, a combination of question and statement.

"I'm a bit rusty, but it's surprising how quickly it comes back once you start using it again."

"Kinda like jumping back in the saddle after a long dry spell."

There was no mistaking the innuendo in Tate's comment. An itch of arousal skidded over Victoria's shoulders and down her back and settled uncomfortably between her legs. She wanted to counter with an equally witty reply but her brain had other ideas. Finally Tate filled the silence.

"Where did you learn to speak it?" Tate scooted her chair a little closer to Victoria.

"High school. Everyone else was studying Spanish and I refused to go along with the trend so, to my parents' chagrin, I took French." Steam drifted up from her cup just before she took a drink.

"A bit of a maverick in your youth?"

"I didn't think so, but my parents would probably say otherwise." Victoria pictured the faces of her parents.

"Where did you grow up that Spanish was all the rage?" Tate stirred a packet of sugar into her steaming cup.

Victoria tucked a strand of hair behind her ear. "San Antonio."

Tate laughed. "I can see why there's not much call for French in a state that borders Mexico."

"That's exactly what my parents said. But they let me take it anyway and I fell in love with it after the first class. Four years in high school and another four in college."

"You went to UCLA, right?" Tate blew on her cappuccino before she took a tentative sip.

"That's right."

"We were practically neighbors. I was at Ohio State."

"You consider twenty-two hundred miles as neighbors?"

This time Victoria laughed. "Even if we had been, I'm sure I was long gone by the time you got to college." Victoria had often speculated on their age difference, guessing it was closer to twenty years than ten.

"You're not much older than I am," Tate replied.

"I'm sure I am."

"Prove it."

Tate's tone was more inquisitive than demanding. She was obviously fishing for Victoria's age so Victoria answered. "I'm forty-four."

"I never would have guessed. I would have said mid to late thirties."

"Flattery will get you another cup of cappuccino." Victoria caught the waiter's eye.

"What would I get if I said you have amazing blue eyes?"

Victoria's stomach flipped and she struggled to keep her expression neutral. She took a calming breath. "You'd get a polite 'thank you.'"

Tate visibly relaxed. "Better that than a slap in the face."

"Do you often get slapped?" Victoria was teasing, trying to make Tate smile.

Tate shook her head and thought a minute. "Thankfully, no. I usually know what the woman's reaction will be beforehand." The women she was drawn to were usually her age or younger with the same uncommitted position as hers. She didn't view herself a player, or a slut, for that matter. She saw herself as more of a realist, and when she wanted the company of a woman or needed to touch another soft warm body, she did. Nothing overly complicated or debauched about it.

But Victoria was different. She was poised, sophisticated, sure of herself in a very sexy, sensuous way. Her hair looked soft and thick, she was always impeccably groomed, and the clothes she was wearing even as a tourist whispered sophistication. Tate's dates weren't trash, but certainly not like Victoria either.

Earlier, Tate had been sitting by the window in a café not far from her hotel when she saw Victoria walking down the sidewalk across the street. She almost hadn't recognized her. Her blond hair was down and blowing in the light breeze. Her jeans were tucked into flat-heeled knee-high black boots. Silver buckles on the sides glinted in the morning sun. Her dark jacket was zipped to her neck, her hands snugly inside the side pockets. Tate had quickly paid her bill and hurried after her.

She followed at a discreet distance, choosing to observe Victoria instead of making her presence known. Casually Victoria window-shopped and strolled along. She barely glanced at the typical tourist shops, instead spending time in the quaint local boutiques scattered along the cobblestone street. She spent at least thirty minutes in a small leather boutique, exiting with a box bearing the logo of the store. The box was large and Tate wondered what she had bought. She had followed Victoria into the square and suddenly wanted to spend more time with her. Tate had surprised herself by asking if she could join her.

The waiter brought the bill and Tate reached for it. "My treat. After all, I invited myself into your quiet moment." She dropped the required Euros on the table. "Wanna play tourist with me? I promise no pictures. I hate being in cities by myself. Especially one so steeped in history." She knew she was babbling, with a touch of BS thrown in, but she didn't want Victoria to leave. "Besides, you can translate for me." Most of the shopkeepers spoke French.

"What did you have in mind?" Victoria asked, obviously cautious.

"May I?" Tate reached for Victoria's map. "We could start with the places around here. There's the museum, the town hall, and all the shopping. After our feet get tired we can have lunch over there and figure out what to do next." Tate pointed to another outdoor patio.

After a few moments, during which Victoria unaccountably flushed, she said, "All right. You're in charge of the map."

Tate quickly helped Victoria into her jacket. Victoria grabbed the package she had bought earlier and followed Tate off the raised platform toward the museum.

Two hours later, they were walking down one of the streets that spoked off from the Grand Place. Victoria stopped in front of a small shop and studied the display of lace in the front window.

"Wanna go inside?" Tate asked.

"I don't want to bore you with my souvenir shopping." Victoria started to move on.

"I wouldn't be bored. Isn't that what being a tourist is all about? Shopping?" Tate hated shopping as much as she hated her annual physical, but both were necessary. It was obvious that Victoria wanted to go inside, and at that moment Tate wanted to do nothing but give Victoria what she wanted.

"Come on." Tate opened the door and stepped inside the small, musty shop.

"Bonjour. May I help you?" An old woman Tate guessed to be in her seventies appeared from a narrow doorway.

Victoria spoke to the woman in French, and she quickly disappeared through the door she emerged from.

"What did you ask her?" Victoria had been translating all morning.

"If she had something special as a gift for my mother."

The woman returned before Tate had a chance to say anything else. She watched closely as Victoria gently touched the lace. She and the woman spoke quietly, their heads bowed in concentration. Several times the woman went back through the mysterious doorway, each time returning with another piece that Victoria inspected. Finally Victoria selected the one she wanted and the woman disappeared with her selection again.

"Is that a tablecloth?" Tate hated to sound so ignorant, but she was way out of her league with this kind of stuff.

"Yes." Victoria searched through her backpack.

"How did you know what size?" *God, what a stupid question.*

"I was with my mom when she bought the table. We must have gone to every furniture store in Texas before she found what she was looking for. Weirdest vacation I ever had."

The expression on Victoria's face was happy, even if her last comment was sarcastic. Tate flashed on her mother and father and quickly shut the thought down.

"What was so special about this shop? We must have passed a dozen shops that sell lace tablecloths."

"Because everything in here is handmade. The woman creates everything in the back." Victoria indicated the door that the woman had disappeared into. "Nothing is mass produced on a machine in here."

"You handled it as if it were a treasure," Tate said carefully.

"Isn't it?" Victoria replied as if it were the most obvious answer in the world.

Tate was about to say something else, but the old woman returned with Victoria's purchase in a plain brown bag.

Victoria handed over her credit card, and after doing some quick math, Tate was stunned by the amount she paid. *A treasure indeed.*

"Tell me about her," Tate asked as they stepped back out onto the cobblestone street.

"My mother?"

Tate nodded.

"She's a nurse. She keeps threatening to retire but my dad won't let her."

"Why not?" A wave of melancholy washed over Tate as Victoria fondly spoke about her parents. She had nothing but bad memories, all of them involving screaming, slapping, and other assorted forms of bruising bodily contact. Her father was a mean drunk, taking out his frustrations on those closest to him even if it meant climbing the stairs and dragging her out of bed to hammer on.

"He says she'll have too many honey-do's for him if she sits home all day. Like my mother would sit home all day." Victoria laughed and, like a woman on a mission, headed straight for a tacky souvenir shop.

"And speaking of my dad, he'll love this tie." Victoria held it up to show her and started laughing. "This is my dad all right. He speaks to the world through his ties. He says they reflect parts of his personality he can't usually show. He's an accountant," Victoria explained. "This is perfect. It'll be his way of saying 'piss on the world.'"

The tie was dark blue with dozens of images of the famed statue "Manneken Pis" on it, each one about half an inch tall. The fountain depicting a naked little boy urinating into the fountain's basin was a famous landmark in Brussels.

"Do you buy something for your parents everywhere you go?"

"No, but Belgium is famous for its lace and the 'Manneken Pis.' Who can resist?" Victoria handed the clerk twenty Euros. After she got her change, she looked at Tate. "How about some lunch?"

They ate at the De Gulden Boot and sat outside facing the square. While Victoria studied her menu, Tate studied her. When she first met Victoria, her height was the only thing she saw. Now after several meetings and spending the morning together, Tate had discovered so much more.

In addition to Victoria's stunning beauty, she treated everyone she met with respect. Clayton could take a lesson from her, Tate thought. Victoria had a fabulous sense of humor. One minute she was totally serious as she studied a painting; the next she was making a wisecrack about all the fruit in another. She was bright and witty, and she obviously loved her parents. If only Tate could say the same about hers. Tate hadn't spoken to or seen her father since high school, and she had no idea if he was even still alive. She doubted it but had no desire to waste her time finding out.

As they sipped their third cappuccino of the day, Tate took her first good look at the square. She had totally focused on

Victoria when she was here earlier, and barely glanced at her surroundings. Lights strung across the square from corner to corner lit up the space under the overcast sky. Tate was no expert, but she thought the lighting detracted from the natural beauty of the buildings. It probably provided much-needed illumination, but seemed too commercial.

"What do you think?" Victoria's voice drew her back from her study of the ancient buildings.

"I'm sorry. What do I think about what?" Tate shifted her full attention to Victoria and spotted a small drip of foam on her upper lip. "You have some whipped cream right here." Tate wiped the offending cream off Victoria's lip with her thumb before she had a chance to use her napkin.

The instant she touched Victoria's lips, Tate's body lit up, as if on fire. Heat ran from her thumb to her toes, settling in that special place in the middle. She cupped Victoria's cheek, her fingers disappearing into the thick warm hair.

Their eyes locked and the square was suddenly soundless. The sounds of laughing children, people talking, and the soft rumble of the storm clouds vanished. The only thing that existed was Victoria. Tate didn't know if she was breathing or not. If not and she died, the feel of Victoria's warm, soft lips would be the last thing she remembered.

Victoria barely had time to register what Tate said before she touched her. Her skin burned, then tingled under Tate's soft hand. The look in Tate's eyes took her breath away. Pure desire was staring back at her, and she had no doubt that Tate wanted her. A rush of pleasure warmed her. It had been a long time since someone had looked at her like that, especially someone as young and vibrant as Tate.

For a few moments she basked in the feeling before she gathered her wits and remembered that Tate stood between her and Braxton. Tate was her adversary, not someone to take as a holiday lover. Victoria broke eye contact first and spoke to Tate, who looked as distracted as Victoria felt.

"I asked if you wanted an authentic Belgian waffle for dessert."

"Sounds good." Tate's hand seemed to be shaking when she removed it from Victoria's face. She stumbled getting out of her chair and cursed when she banged her knee on the table leg.

Tate followed Victoria out of the square and as they walked by a shop Tate froze. In the window stood a mannequin wearing a black thong, red-and-black garter belt, black fishnet stockings, and next-to-nothing bra. Other equally revealing lingerie with either more or less lace filled the rest of the window.

"Tate? Are you all right?" Victoria glanced around to see what she was staring at and also froze when she realized what it was. "Oh, my," Victoria murmured.

The sexy and provocative lingerie was obviously doing to Tate exactly what it was designed to do. She seemed so dazed Victoria almost had to shake her to get her attention.

Without taking her eyes off the sight, Tate asked, "Wanna go in *there*?"

"I don't think that would be a good idea." This was the first time Victoria had dared acknowledge the sexual attraction between them.

Victoria walked away, hoping Tate would follow. She wasn't that lucky. After murmuring what sounded to Victoria like "I do," Tate stepped inside. Victoria had two choices, stay outside like a prude or follow her and pretend the blatant sexual display didn't bother her. She chose the latter and failed miserably.

The inside of the shop was more provocative than the window. An oversized poster of a dark-haired woman clad in a bustier and garter belt dominated the wall adjacent to the door. Everywhere Victoria looked, bras, panties, corsets, and other lingerie were displayed in all their glory. The garments were not the type she had seen in the adult shops, the crotchless undies and nipple-baring bras. These were sexy without being slutty.

Tate wandered around the store, almost caressing the fabric and lace. Victoria flushed, imagining Tate touching her that way.

Victoria was in no way a prude and had several pairs of equally sexy lingerie in her drawer at home. But being in this shop with Tate was unnerving, especially after what happened at lunch. She didn't want to think of Tate that way but couldn't stand this close to her and not do so.

"Do you intend to buy anything?" Victoria was horrified at her question. So much for restraint.

Tate studied her, dark green eyes tracing a slow path over every curve on her body. Victoria felt as if she was being physically stroked and her nipples hardened in response.

Tate locked eyes with her. "Not for me."

Her voice was low and husky, and Victoria suddenly felt very, very warm. Vivid images of half-naked sweaty bodies intertwined and rubbing together clouded her mind. "I'll wait outside."

A few minutes later Victoria felt Tate's breath on her ear before she spoke. "I'm ready for that dessert now."

Between the touch at lunch, the lingerie shop, and Tate's suggestive mention of dessert, Victoria couldn't say a word. She let Tate take her arm and lead her down the street.

Chapter Twelve

Victoria was vividly aware of Tate's possessive grip on her arm or her hand on the small of her back, which on more than one occasion kept her from getting trampled by over-eager tourists looking through their viewfinder instead of where they were going. The bag in Tate's hand bumped into her once or twice and Victoria wondered not only what she had bought but for whom.

They reached a small food court where Victoria immediately smelled what they were looking for.

"My treat," Tate said, leading her to an empty table under a striped umbrella. "Looks like you have your choice of dessert smothered in chocolate or strawberries and with or without whipped cream."

Tate's reading of the menu was seductive and sensuous. Something down low came to life and Victoria had trouble forming her answer. This time when she looked into Tate's eyes they weren't filled with desire but with a teasing twinkle that almost dared her to take the bait. Victoria knew a test when she saw one and calmly replied, "Chocolate, of course. With whipped cream."

Victoria watched Tate make her way through the line to the counter. Victoria always traveled alone and took in as many of the local sights as she had time for. Unfortunately, touring alone with no one to share the experience with was almost like masturbating. *Masturbating! Where in the hell did that come from?* She felt her face flush and covered up her discomfort with a fake cough.

Her mind was running in a hundred directions, and she didn't want to go in any of them. She had been aware of Tate's every movement from the time she showed up this morning, and after Tate touched her at lunch, the sensations heightened. Tate's fingers were soft, almost caressing, and the fire in her eyes flared.

Victoria wanted Tate's touch to continue, but she had to stop any further advances. They were adversaries, fighting for control over a multi-billion-dollar company. It didn't get more serious than that. Drake was fighting for its life, and whatever the outcome, it would be her legacy. The burden was overwhelming, and for just a moment, she was tempted to give in. She was flattered by Tate's attraction to her and admittedly more than a little horny, but that was no excuse for mixing business with pleasure.

She caught herself doing it again. Imagining how Tate's body would feel under hers. Or would she take control and their positions would be reversed. *Who cares?* She envisioned sweat dripping off Tate's strong jaw or sliding down between her breasts.

Tate looked over her shoulder and her small knowing smile let Victoria know she had been caught. She changed chairs, needing to sit with her back to Tate to control her wayward thoughts. The people walking in all directions on the street in front of her grabbed her attention. She caught snippets of German and French, and an occasional British accent.

"Here you go, one authentic Belgian waffle covered in authentic Belgian chocolate. You look like a whipped-cream woman, so I got you extra." Tate put the plate, fork, and napkins on the table and sat down across from her.

Tate had felt Victoria's eyes on her while she was in line and couldn't resist looking at her. A rush of excitement filled her when she had caught Victoria totally focused on her. Women eyed her all the time with more than a little interest, but none made her feel the way she did when Victoria did the same thing. She felt hot, tender, and powerful all at the same time.

"Thanks. It looks delicious." Victoria slid the plate closer. Her finger slipped into the chocolate and Tate's breathing stopped when her tongue darted out to lick it off. She couldn't help but focus on Victoria's mouth as her tongue disappeared. She desperately wanted to kiss her and leaned forward to do just that, though she realized what she was doing and stopped herself before Victoria noticed. But what if she did? What would Victoria do? Would she back away or make that ever-so-slight motion to indicate her kiss would be welcome? Suddenly Tate wanted to find out, and this time when she ventured toward Victoria she didn't stop herself.

Victoria's lips were soft and warm. For an instant they were still, and then began to move subtly against hers. She tasted like chocolate and cream, and Tate wanted more. She increased the pressure of the kiss for a second, then pulled back, separating their lips by a mere heartbeat. Victoria didn't close the gap or move away. Their breath mixed and electricity crackled around them. Finally, Victoria stepped away.

"I don't think you should do that again." Her voice was soft but not very convincing.

"Why? Didn't you like it?" Victoria had kissed her with equal passion so Tate knew the answer to the question.

"Because I don't want you to do it again." Victoria's normally straightforward gaze was anywhere but directed at her.

"Why?" Tate repeated her question. This time Victoria *did* look at her, and Tate recognized the desire burning in her blue eyes.

"Because I don't mix business with pleasure," Victoria said, more firmly this time.

"And you think being with me would be pleasurable?" Tate teased. She liked the fact that Victoria was slightly off-kilter. It was sweet.

"I don't need to answer that question, Tate. It's obvious there's something between us, but I am not going to let it happen. We're here to work, not play."

Victoria took a deep breath, fighting her own desires. At this moment she wished her sense of propriety was a lot less strict than it was. She wanted nothing more than to drag Tate into a dark doorway and kiss her all afternoon. She had known Tate was going to kiss her and had done nothing to stop it. In fact, when Tate's head dipped again, she lifted her chin a fraction of an inch just before their lips met.

Tate's lips were hot and persuasive. She demanded participation so subtly that Victoria couldn't help but comply. When Tate's tongue traced the outline of her lips, she was afraid she would melt in her chair. She hadn't wanted the kiss to end but secretly was glad it did. She didn't know how much more strength she possessed.

"I can do both." Tate sounded somewhat cocky.

"So can I, but I choose not to and I hope you will respect that." Victoria's conviction was returning.

"And if I don't?"

"Then you may find your face slapped," Victoria countered.

Tate looked at her for several long moments before she settled back in her chair. "All right, Victoria. I don't believe you for a second, but I'll behave."

Looking at the mischievous glint in Tate's eyes, Victoria didn't believe her either.

Tate insisted on walking her back to her hotel. Victoria was booked at the Sheraton and had no idea where Tate was staying. She told herself she didn't want to know. If she didn't know, she wouldn't be tempted to knock on her door later tonight.

What was going on with her? She'd had other woman hit on her as blatantly as Tate. She should have made time to see Carole before she left. Maybe that would have taken the edge off. Then again, as sexy and attractive as Tate was, she doubted it would have helped.

They strolled down the street, Tate carrying most of the conversation. Victoria was vaguely aware of what Tate was saying, but her body was totally aware of everything about her. She stood tall when she walked, as if she owned the sidewalk. Her stride was sure and easily kept up with Victoria's. Their arms touched as they walked and Victoria didn't really care if it was intentional on Tate's part or accidental. When Tate mentioned guns, Victoria paid attention.

"You'd never see this in the States. A gun store smack between a temporary staffing agency and a sandwich shop." Tate had stepped back to see the adjacent stores, but Victoria focused on what was behind the window.

"Wow, a Walther Nighthawk. It even has a scope." She couldn't keep the excitement from her voice.

"You know guns?"

"My father taught me to shoot when I was ten years old. We'd go out to the desert or to the gun range and spend all day practicing." Those were the times Victoria would always remember. When it came time for her dad's eulogy that's what she would talk about. They had a connection that began when she was a little girl and only grew stronger. She loved being her father's daughter.

"My father would probably shoot *at* me instead of *with* me," Tate replied blandly.

Victoria pulled her attention from the weapons behind the thick glass and gazed at Tate. She didn't say anything.

Tate shrugged. "Guess I was lucky he couldn't scrape together two nickels to buy one."

She resumed walking down the street and Victoria had to hurry to catch up. She didn't know what to say. At first she thought Tate was kidding, but her expression told Victoria she was serious. The pain appeared for only an instant before it disappeared behind a carefully constructed mask. But she had seen it briefly and her heart ached for the troubled childhood Tate had alluded to several times.

"I had a great time today. Thanks for inviting yourself along. It wouldn't have been half as interesting if I'd been alone," Victoria said. They were waiting at a stop light across the street from her hotel.

"Yeah, someone else might have kissed you."

Victoria's heart jumped into her throat at Tate's reference to their kiss in the middle of town. During the entire walk back she had thought of nothing other than the way Tate's lips felt. She couldn't get it off her mind, which wasn't good. She looked at Tate and the crowd around them surged forward, catching them up in the movement. She stumbled off the curb but Tate caught her with a sure hand before she could fall.

"I doubt that," Victoria finally replied as they arrived at the revolving door to the Sheraton.

"Why do you say that? You're a beautiful woman and any lesbian in her right mind would want to kiss you. Actually she'd want to do more than just kiss you, believe me." Tate chuckled.

Tate's light banter only inflamed her tight nerves. "And are you in your right mind?" she couldn't help but ask.

Tate studied her, searching her eyes for something before she replied softly, "Yes, I am," then closed the distance between them again.

Tate put her hand behind her neck and pulled Victoria's head down. She knew Tate was about to kiss her again and did nothing to stop her. Her mind was fighting a battle of intellect but her body was winning the war. When their lips met Victoria wrapped her arms around Tate and pulled her close. Tate responded by opening her mouth in invitation for her to do the same. She eagerly accepted. Their tongues met and Victoria's stomach dropped and her knees almost buckled. The kiss wasn't sloppy or terribly inappropriate for a street corner in the middle of Europe, but it was the most passionate one Victoria had ever experienced.

Slowly she slid her hands down Tate's neck and rested them on her chest. She didn't have to apply much pressure for Tate to release her lips. Victoria couldn't meet her eyes when she whispered, "I'm not."

❖

Tate watched Victoria enter the lobby and kept her eyes on her as long as she could. She was tempted to follow her and continue what they started on the street, but thought better of it. She had often changed women's minds for her own gratification, but for some odd reason pressuring Victoria seemed tacky and cheap. Like what she had done when Victoria was helpless in Phoenix. Victoria would shoot her if she knew she had taken advantage of her illness and copied all the information in her briefcase. At the time she had experienced no remorse about doing it, but now she felt uncharacteristically guilty.

She reversed her direction and walked back the way they had come, not paying much attention to her surroundings. Her thoughts were full of Victoria. The way she smelled, the way she tasted, the tentative then aggressive way she kissed her. Tate was concentrating so much on her that she walked past her hotel and had to backtrack when she realized what she had done. Her stomach growled but she wasn't really interested in eating. She went directly to her room and stripped off her clothes and stepped into the shower.

Fifteen minutes later she wrapped herself in the thick terry-cloth robe provided by the hotel and ordered room service. The light on the phone was blinking, indicating she had a message, and her heart jumped when she immediately thought it might be Victoria. It just as quickly fell when she remembered that she had not told Victoria where she was staying. She punched in the code and listened.

Clayton had called several times, each time more anxious and demanding than the last. She checked her watch. It was just after two in the afternoon at home, and for the first time ever, Tate didn't feel up to dealing with him, which surprised her. Clayton Sumner had always energized her. She fed off his energy, his determination, and his take-no-prisoners style. He was a typical Type-A personality, and in her own way, Tate was molding herself in his image.

Before this deal she would have returned Clayton's call regardless of the time difference; he expected it. But not tonight. She wanted to relive her day with Victoria. She wanted to imprint the feelings and experience in her brain so she would never forget them. She couldn't remember ever having such an enjoyable time with a woman outside of sex. Then again, she tried to recall the last time she even did anything with a woman, other than have sex. She couldn't, and for some reason that lack made her feel sad. Here she was thirty-three years old, her world on a string that she controlled, and she was thinking about a woman who was more woman than she had ever known.

Tate was scared. Victoria was out of her league. She was successful, complex, classy, and refined. What was she thinking coming on to her? At first it had been a challenge to see if she could get her into bed, but soon it became an almost uncontrollable need. She paced in front of her hotel-room window, the lights of the city twinkling below her. They reminded her of the light in Victoria's eyes when she talked about her parents or something she was interested in.

Tate clenched her fists in frustration. What was wrong with her? She had never been so hung up on a woman. She wanted to know everything about Victoria, get inside her and never come out. She saw her own reflection in the glass and didn't recognize the stranger.

Chapter Thirteen

Victoria slapped at the alarm and silenced the obnoxious buzz. Hotel alarm clocks had the most awful sounds specifically designed to wake the dead. She definitely felt dead this morning. She had barely slept the night before, her dreams a tangle of images, most of them of one specific dark-haired woman. She woke in the middle of one very vivid dream and stopped fighting the need to bring herself to climax while she fantasized Tate whispering naughty words in her ear. Pushing aside her guilt at masturbating over her main rival, she tossed back the covers and staggered toward the shower.

While the water heated, she ordered a pot of coffee and caught her reflection in the mirror. Dark circles surrounded her normally clear eyes, and her face was puffy. She would have to put in some extra work to look alive this morning before she faced Tate and Peter Braxton.

The limo was scheduled to meet her at eight, and she had been waiting outside for fifteen minutes when it pulled up. She cursed herself every time she looked up and down the street in search of Tate. She was acting like a love-struck teenager, for God's sake. The drive to Braxton's factory took twenty-five minutes, and they reached the wide drive just before eight thirty.

A Town Car was parked in front of them, its driver opening the rear passenger door. Victoria caught her breath when Tate stepped out, her long legs covered by her coat that hung below her knees and a scarf wrapped around her neck to defend her from the unseasonably bitter cold that had invaded Brussels that morning. She pulled her briefcase from the car, then thanked the driver and looked around as if sizing up her newly acquired company.

"Ma'am?" Victoria's driver asked.

"I'm sorry, give me just a minute." Victoria didn't want to face Tate right now. She needed time to control her breathing and try to calm her racing heart. Tate stared at her car, but Victoria knew she couldn't see her through the dark tint on the windows. After a few moments, Tate went inside.

Victoria drank several swallows of water, taking a deep breath between each. She glanced at her watch and with one last swallow opened the door. As the wind hit her face like pin pricks of ice, her eyes began to tear. She quickly grabbed her own briefcase and hurried through the front door. She didn't want to appear at the meeting with a runny nose and watery eyes. How unprofessional would that be? And with Tate in the room with her for the entire day, she needed every ounce of control she could muster.

The guard checked her name off a list on his clipboard and escorted her to the elevator, then waited for her to step inside. He punched the button for the second floor and wished her a good day. Victoria checked herself in the mirrors on the elevator doors and was just unbuttoning her coat when the doors opened. The smell of rich coffee hit her nostrils as she stepped out into the vestibule.

"Ms. Sosa, good morning. I'm Amy, Mr. Braxton's assistant here in Brussels. May I take your coat?"

"Thank you." Victoria was impressed by the poise of the young woman, who was at least a foot shorter than she was. Most women couldn't help gawking momentarily before they remembered their manners. Amy didn't seem the least bit fazed. Perhaps Braxton had briefed her.

"This way please," Amy said, after she hung up Victoria's coat. "Ms. Monroe is already here and Mr. Braxton will be with you in a minute. He's on a call right now but won't be long. There is coffee and water in the conference room. Can I get you anything else?"

Victoria replied in French, "No, thank you, that won't be necessary." Amy smiled broadly.

Tate was standing, looking out the window, her back to the door but she turned when Victoria spoke to Amy. Their eyes met and all the air seemed to have been sucked out of the room. She didn't hear Amy close the door behind her.

Tate was wearing black pleated trousers topped with a bright green shirt tucked in at the waist. Her belt was wide and funky, and she had on a pair of clunky black boots. She looked nothing like someone bidding on a multi-billion-dollar company. In contrast, Victoria wore navy slacks with a pale blue shell and contrasting jacket. She felt old and dowdy while Tate looked like she had just stepped off the campus of any Ivy League school in the country. She looked deliciously handsome, just as she had in Victoria's dream last night.

Tate's expression gave nothing away when she said good morning, but her eyes danced with desire. *Oh, God. It's way too early in the morning for this.*

Victoria put her briefcase down on the floor beside a chair and crossed the room to the gleaming stainless coffeepot on the credenza. "Good morning," she said, pouring a cup of hot coffee. "Thank God, the real thing instead of the instant stuff." The cup rattled on the saucer and she grasped them with her other hand, more nervous than she thought.

"Sleep well?" Tate asked.

Victoria hadn't heard Tate move, but the deep voice came from just over her right shoulder. Tate was standing much closer than Victoria wanted her to be. She stepped away toward the safety of her chair. "Yes, thank you." She didn't dare return the question. Who knew where Tate would take any reference to night and beds. She chided herself. A woman as sexual and sensuous as Tate didn't need darkness or a bed.

"I didn't," she replied, not waiting for Victoria to ask. "I kept dreaming of waffles, chocolate, and a beautiful blonde."

Victoria's hand was in her briefcase and she froze midway from pulling out a sheaf of papers. The look of desire in Tate's eyes hadn't dimmed, and Victoria's blood began to race so loud she thought everyone in the building could hear it. She remained motionless as Tate stepped closer.

"It looks like you didn't get much sleep either."

Victoria's legs trembled and she rested her thighs against the hard table for support. She had no idea why she was so drawn to Tate. She was brash and a cutthroat in business, not minding who or what she left in her path. She was much younger and so comfortable with her sexuality she didn't appear to give a shit what anyone thought of her. She was very different from any woman Victoria had ever been attracted to.

Thankfully, Tate didn't come any closer, and Victoria pulled herself out of the tempting abyss when Peter Braxton entered the room.

"Ladies, good morning." Braxton didn't appear to notice the tension or the fact that Tate was standing inches from her. Four people followed him into the room and he quickly made introductions.

Victoria forced herself to concentrate on each man's name and his function at Braxton Europe. She had to convince these men, as well as Peter, that Drake was the company to sell to. They settled into their seats and began their presentations.

Each man took an hour to review the financials, market trends, industry reports, and people issues for his respective business unit. Victoria took notes to keep her mind from drifting to Tate, who sat beside her.

The morning passed quickly and over lunch they all continued their conversation, with both Tate and her asking follow-up questions. All too soon they were back in the conference room for another hour before they donned blue lab coats and headed onto the factory floor.

The afternoon flew by and after they shook hands with Braxton's staff, they affirmed a final agreement to meet in Hong Kong in two days. Crossing the lobby she buttoned her coat, and a blast of bitter-cold wind struck her the instant she stepped outside. Tate was waiting for her and stepped forward when Victoria exited the building and headed toward the car door her driver had opened.

"Have dinner with me?"

Victoria was afraid this would happen, which was why she'd purposely dawdled in the ladies' room upstairs. She didn't want to be forced to come up with a plausible reason to decline. She was exhausted from trying to focus on all of the factors of Braxton Europe she needed to know, and Tate's every movement beside her didn't help. She could say she was flying to Hong Kong this evening, but there weren't many direct flights from Brussels to Hong Kong. She could easily get caught in that fib.

"It's been a long day, Tate, and I'm really tired. All I want to do is go back to the hotel, soak in a hot bath, and order room service." And of course work half the night, but she didn't tell Tate that.

Tate propped herself suggestively against her car. "Can I wash your back?"

"No."

The expression on the driver's face indicated that he was enjoying their conversation.

"Can I at least tuck you in?"

Victoria's frustration jumped to the surface. Her nerves had been overloaded all day, especially the main one between her legs. "No." Victoria slid into the backseat. Before the driver had a chance to close the door, Tate stuck her head inside.

"What do I have to do to get you to say yes?"

There was more in her question than what she was asking. "I'm not going to say yes to what you want, Tate, so you can stop asking." Victoria could smell Tate's cologne, as she had all day.

"But it's what you want too, Victoria. Why deny it?"

"I'm not denying it," Victoria admitted. "I'm simply not acting on it. Now if you'll excuse me." Victoria effectively ended the conversation and her driver closed the door.

Tate watched Victoria's car pull away, an unfamiliar ache filling her chest. She hated that Victoria had gotten under her skin and wasn't about to let it happen again. She pushed the unwelcome sensation aside and told her driver to take her to an American bar.

Two hours later Tate's eyes burned from the cigarette smoke and her body throbbed from thinking about Victoria. Seeing Victoria today had been harder than she thought. She had anticipated feeling some excitement when she was with her again, but nothing had prepared her for her consuming consciousness of Victoria. She couldn't think and could barely pay attention to Braxton and his drones.

"At the risk of sounding clichéd, can I buy you a drink?"

Tate almost laughed at the tired line, but when she saw a stunning redhead slide into the seat beside her she smiled. "As long as you don't expect me to ask you if you come here often." The woman's laugh was genuine and Tate signaled for the bartender.

Tate lifted her glass to indicate another of the same. This would make her third Crown Royal on the rocks. One more on her empty stomach might just make her forget about Victoria.

The redhead made her interest known before she finished her first drink, and Tate was tempted. Maybe a night with another woman would get her mind off Victoria. The woman beside her was more than willing, and Tate knew it would merely be a casual fling.

She was about to say yes when she realized, even in her

alcohol-induced state, that she didn't want sex with a total stranger. She wanted to make love with Victoria, and anyone other than her would be a poor substitute.

"Thanks, and under other circumstances I'd say yes, but this isn't a good time for me." She briefly wondered if there would ever be a good time again.

❖

Victoria's cell phone rang just as she was about to step into the tub. She looked at the caller ID and debated whether to answer, but if she didn't, Edward Hamacher would call all night until he got her. Reluctantly she grabbed the robe from the hook on the back of the door and flipped open her phone.

"Victoria Sosa." She always answered the phone with her full name when he called. She needed to immediately establish power and a sense of professionalism whenever he was concerned.

"Victoria, it's Edward," he said unnecessarily.

"Yes, Edward, what can I do for you?" He wanted an update but she was determined to make him ask for it.

"Where are we?"

She ignored his question and answered instead, "It's just as I expected. They have a very well-run operation here. Braxton has a good executive staff that seems to be on top of everything."

"So you plan to recommend that we close this deal?" He had been trying to get Victoria to commit to buying Braxton from the very first day it was discussed. Victoria had insisted that while Claire and the external auditor were looking at the books, she would be touring the facilities. When and only when all doubts were gone would she make a formal offer to Braxton. Edward was obviously losing patience.

"We've talked about this several times, Edward. I can't in good conscience, let alone fiscally, agree to this merger if I'm not certain it is in our best interest. I am more confident today than I was yesterday, but I still need to see their Asia operations. Claire will be done with the books by the end of the week. We'll have a much better idea then."

"The clock is ticking, Victoria," Edward said menacingly.

"Is there anything else, Edward? I still have a company to run and a million things to do tonight." Unfortunately a relaxing bath was off the list. She was too pissed at him to be able to unwind. Taking a quick shower and tackling her e-mail had moved to the top of the list.

"I'll be waiting for your call, Victoria."

The way he said her name was so condescending she ground her teeth. "I'll report back to the entire board the results of my site visits and the audit as scheduled. Now if there's nothing else, good night, Edward." Victoria hung up the phone far more calmly than she felt. "Bastard," she said to Hamacher's unhearing ears.

For the second time in as many nights, Victoria slept very little. She typed up her notes, including her thoughts on Braxton, while they were still fresh in her mind. The sun was starting to lighten the sky by the time she shut off her laptop. Her eyes were gritty from lack of sleep and her brain was mush. Her legs twitched from inactivity. She decided to go for a short run to relax. Her flight wasn't until two that afternoon, and she could sleep during the fourteen-hour trip to Hong Kong.

Thirty-five minutes later Victoria was breathing heavily and sweating profusely, but her mind was clear. The streets around her hotel were empty this early in the morning, and she ran for a full hour before she returned to her room to shower and pack.

She was proud of herself. She had thought of Tate only half the time. Once her mind was empty of work it was free to drift to more pleasant things, and Tate Monroe was definitely pleasant. Sort of. She was more than pleasant to look at, made her body feel things she had almost forgotten, but she was driving her crazy.

Why couldn't they have met under different circumstances? Victoria laughed to herself. They would have never met. Tate's youth meant they didn't run around in the same social circles. But if they had?

She and Carole weren't committed but casual, getting together whenever they could. She wasn't seeing anyone other than Carole, but that was primarily because she hadn't met anyone she wanted to go out with, let alone have sex with. She thought about the situation for a minute and decided she wouldn't be cheating on Carole if she were to sleep with someone else. She suspected Carole did, but they never talked about it. They never needed to.

Carole was comfortable. She was equally busy, didn't push or make demands on her. Victoria unconsciously compared her to Tate. Tate as a lover would be demanding, exciting, challenging, and would expect the same from her partner. She would be as intense about sex as she was about life. Victoria's heart raced again, but this time not from exercise. Sex with Tate would be astonishing.

❖

Tate's head was splitting and she felt like a train had run over her. Then she remembered the train was named Victoria. Raising her head off the pillow, she groaned as her stomach threatened to empty. Why did she drink so much? Why did she say no to the woman? She rarely declined such an appetizing invitation. At the risk of vomiting, Tate rolled on her stomach and fell back asleep.

Several hours later, after stumbling out of bed after her wake-up call, Tate moved slowly to the shower. Her flight was at six that evening and the car would pick her up at three thirty. That gave her several hours to clean up and get ready, and judging by the way she felt, she would need every minute.

She spent thirty of those minutes simply standing under the warm spray in the shower. She was tempted to use the pulsation head to ease the tension in her groin, but her mind had finally begun to clear, and she didn't want the pounding between her legs to settle in her head again.

Much later, dressed and on the way to the airport, Tate reviewed her itinerary. She would land in Hong Kong early tomorrow, and Clayton would expect her to call before she landed. The day would be similar to yesterday, but with a different cast of characters. Meetings, questions, answers, charts, graphs, and Victoria.

Tate settled into her seat in first class, and once they reached their cruising altitude she called Clayton on the air phone. It was two thirty in the afternoon in New York. She briefed him on some of her additional thoughts about how to clinch the deal from the information she had pilfered from Victoria's briefcase.

While Victoria was ill and sleeping in Phoenix, Tate had opened the case, pulled out everything inside, and hit the mother lode. The latest financials, last month's profit-and-loss report, and a preliminary draft of the report Victoria was preparing on the Braxton deal. Tate had made copies of everything, using the fax/copier in the office section of her suite, and neatly replaced everything exactly where she found it.

Now all she had to do was make her plan work.

Chapter Fourteen

Tate had no clue. Not about what she was doing, not about what she wanted, and certainly not about Victoria. They had been in Hong Kong for three days, and during that time she saw a side of Victoria that had only peeked to the surface in Brussels. Yes, she was bright, inquisitive, and perceptive, but she was also kind, generous with her attention, and respectful of everyone she met.

What were Victoria's staff meetings like? Clayton's were often filled with derogatory comments about competitors and insider information that was questionable as to the source of the facts and how they were obtained. The Sumner rumor mill had designated Tate and her boss as the Jaws of Life—a cross between the predator in the movie *Jaws* and the piece of equipment firemen and rescue squads used to extricate victims from horrific, often metal-bending accidents. She often felt like a shark, circling her prey and watching as it grew weaker and weaker until the opportune time for her to strike. She didn't concern herself with the residual damage her actions caused, just the gratification and financial reward of the kill.

Victoria's meetings, on the other hand, were probably factual and data-based, where *humanity* and *respect* weren't just words on the company Internet site but principles that the employees lived and breathed every day. Tate mulled that over. She scoffed at companies that were, in her opinion, noble to a fault. The fault was that they often couldn't make the tough decisions and failed because of that lack. She, however, had no trouble with that aspect of business, having learned from dual masters—her father and Clayton Sumner.

Yet her growing attraction to a woman ten years older than she was puzzled her. Each time they were together in Hong Kong, Tate found herself studying Victoria. The way she spoke, moved, and cocked her head when she was concentrating. The way her face lit up when she smiled.

Tate had become obsessed with her. She had scoured the Internet, gathering every article that even mentioned Victoria's name. She consumed every ounce of information on Victoria and felt as if she had known her for years instead of weeks. Every commentary, critique, and exposé all provoked the same conclusion: Victoria Sosa was a woman of substance, style, composure, kindness, and a keen business sense. At one point Tate toyed with the idea of doing the same research on herself, but there would be no comparison. Absolutely no comparison. At times Victoria scared her.

How had Victoria become so successful? How had she managed to rise to the top of her field and still be admired by everyone? Hadn't everyone left a body or two by the side of the road on their climb up? Tate surely had, and in some cases they were piled pretty high. She had always believed that honor was an accepted casualty of success. Didn't nice guys always finish last? Victoria obviously missed that lesson in business school, whereas Tate had earned the highest mark in class.

The more Tate read and learned about Victoria, the more the picture of who she thought Victoria was changed. She didn't appear to have any major character flaws; her personality was warm and engaging no matter what she was doing or who she was doing it with. Several articles boldly stated that she had the qualities of a true leader, and they were absolutely correct.

Tate reclined in her seat as she returned from Hong Kong

to Atlanta. What a team they would make. Dinner had just been cleared, and the flight attendants were offering coffee to her and the other first-class passengers. With her guts and determination and Victoria's reputation, they could have any business they wanted. They would be the most powerful couple in the business world. Tate pictured their faces on the cover of *Fortune* and *Money* magazines. They would be quoted in the *Wall Street Journal* and the subject of an article in the *Harvard Business Review*. Tate Monroe would become a household name right next to Warren Buffet and Bill Gates.

❖

Shit was the first word that came to mind when Victoria stepped through the front door of the Mason Club. Her neighbor had mentioned coming here when it first opened and it had become *the* go-to place in Atlanta. The lights were low and she immediately knew this wasn't a restaurant where people discussed business. Unless, of course, you were "getting down to business." This meeting was already on her calendar when she arrived at the office after her return from Hong Kong. If she had any idea the atmosphere was designed more for lovers than business associates, she would have insisted on a different place entirely.

The maître d' escorted her to a small table tucked into a corner. Lisa Billings stood as she approached, and even in the dim light, Victoria could see the banker's eyes move slowly over her body. The expression on her face said that she very much liked what she saw. Victoria didn't need this in her life right now. The added complication of tactfully declining Lisa's apparent invitation would be tricky. Obviously she hadn't made it clear that she meant it when she said she didn't mix business with pleasure. She didn't want to alienate Lisa, nor did she want to give her any opening she could run with.

"Victoria, you look fabulous," Lisa said, taking her hand,

and Victoria was surprised when she pulled her in and gave her a quick kiss on the cheek.

We are definitely not going to talk about profit, loss, or pricing strategy tonight. "Thank you. I'm sorry I'm late. I made the mistake of answering the phone before I left."

Lisa laughed in understanding. "Yes, I know how that is. Would you like some wine?" She signaled the waiter.

"No, I prefer water with lemon," she said, addressing the hovering waiter.

Victoria was grateful that Lisa kept the conversation going throughout dinner. They talked about the theater, which team would win the World Series this year, and how angry they both were when Proposition 8 passed in California. Lisa said that her best friend had gotten married in San Francisco shortly after the California Supreme Court ruling allowing gays and lesbians to marry but now didn't know if she was married or not.

Somewhere in the middle of dinner, Victoria changed from water to wine, and by the time they finished she had consumed three glasses of the sweet liquor. Lisa made her interest in Victoria clear, and as the evening wore on she had more and more difficulty wondering why she shouldn't take her up on the offer. She had been thinking of Tate far too often in the two weeks since she'd left her in Hong Kong. She compared every woman she saw to her young adversary. Over dessert she decided that maybe she needed a diversion to get Tate off her mind. It had been a long time since someone other than Tate wanted her. What harm could it do? They were two consenting adults who found each other attractive. They were mature enough to understand what it was and, most importantly, what it wasn't.

"Lisa." Victoria was suddenly nervous. She couldn't remember the last time she propositioned a woman and searched for the words. She certainly couldn't say something as base as "let's go back to your place and fuck." However close to the truth that was, it was still tacky.

"Okay, Victoria, I give up." Lisa leaned back in her chair

and put her hands up in surrender. "I've tried everything to let you know how interested I am in you, but I respect your position about us. I don't like it. I think we could have had something really hot. But I understand, and I promise I'll leave you alone from now on."

"What?" Victoria couldn't believe her luck. She was a breath away from making her move and she got shot down. She didn't know whether to be relieved or frustrated.

"We'll keep it totally professional. I'm sorry if I made you uncomfortable. That wasn't my intention." Lisa looked embarrassed.

"You didn't. I appreciate it. Things can get sticky…" Victoria didn't know what else to say.

"How about we just forget this all happened and next time it'll be lunch in a brightly lit crowded café?" Lisa flagged the waiter for more coffee. "Tell me about Braxton and what you're thinking now that you've seen his operations."

❖

"Aren't you Tate Monroe, the corporate raider? Didn't I see you on *Sixty Minutes* a few months ago?"

Tate lifted her head and looked at the woman who stood beside her table. She was the same one who had been eyeing her for the past hour across the crowded dance floor. Tate wondered if and when she would make a move. She was a knockout, Tate decided as she swung her gaze up from tan bare legs over perky breasts and into big brown eyes. The woman was looking at her like an eager puppy waiting for some sign of acceptance.

"Yes, I am but no, I wasn't on *Sixty Minutes*. And I prefer to think of myself as a successful businesswoman." She was judging the chances of scoring with the blonde who was looking down at her. The woman had potential. "Would you like to sit down?"

Several drinks and two hours later Tate had completely revised her opinion of the woman. Her name was Joni Roseville, and not only did she have a body made to be coveted, but ambition to be reckoned with. The best thing was that Ms. Roseville, as Tate preferred to call her, had insider information on Drake Pharmaceuticals and was in a big hurry to unload it in exchange for a position working for Tate. Ms. Roseville laid out the information in specific, no-misunderstanding detail over cappuccino at the coffee house across the street from the bar.

Tate eyed her carefully before she spoke. "And where did you get this information?" Tate didn't care if the woman had gained it illegally. That wasn't Tate's problem because she didn't do it.

"I worked for people who know some of the bigwigs involved," she answered vaguely.

"And I'm just supposed to believe everything you say?"

"It's the truth," Joni replied, appearing slightly insulted.

Tate was careful, very careful. She had used similar tactics to infiltrate companies where she wanted more information than she could get from official sources. "And I'm supposed to go on faith that what you have is what I need?" The woman had known enough about the Braxton deal to tell Tate she might in fact have vital data.

"You know it goes both ways. What will I do if you don't give me a job after I tell you? Who'll be shit out of luck then? Seems as though I have more to lose than you do."

The woman's demeanor had subtly changed from ditzy blonde to sharp and calculating. Tate wouldn't misjudge the potential for success as well as the significant damage if she didn't handle this situation the right way.

"Why don't we meet in the middle? You give me enough that I know you have what I need, and I'll find a place for you at Sumner. Once that's settled, you give me the rest and I'll make sure you're taken care of." Tate could use a woman like this on her new team. Someone who wasn't afraid to get information and knew what to do with it once she had it. In a way she reminded her of herself when she was just starting out.

"Do we have a deal?" Tate extended her hand across the Formica tabletop. The woman hesitated and Tate was uncertain if she would accept her proposal. She held her gaze steady on the brown eyes, determined to stay on top of the situation. After several seconds, the woman shook it.

❖

Victoria drove home thinking only about crawling into bed. Even though the evening with Lisa didn't end the way she had originally intended, it still took a lot out of her. She had done nothing but eat, sleep, and think about Braxton for the past three months, and she was exhausted. Being around Tate as much as she had during their tour of the Braxton facilities had put her in a constant state of arousal, and as much as she didn't want to react the way she did, she couldn't stop herself. Tate was sexy, and Victoria wanted her. She wanted to know what her skin felt like under her fingers, how soft the underside of her breasts were, how her sweat tasted, and how her arousal smelled. Victoria hadn't desired someone this much in so long she couldn't even remember who it had been.

Tate was everything she should not have. She was far too young and definitely professional suicide. But something about her enticed Victoria, even from the first time they met, and to her horror and surprise, it kept pulling her. Tate was nothing like the women she was usually attracted to. Tate was a free spirit, hot tempered, quick to act, and from what Victoria had seen, she flew by the seat of her pants. She was intense, confident to the point of being cocky, and aggressive. Victoria's women, on the other hand, were easygoing and self-assured, and she was always the one who did the chasing.

She didn't know whether to be flattered or feel old that a woman at least ten years her junior was interested in her. Had she become some pathetic, single, over-forty-four-year-old woman desperate for attention? She didn't think so. God, she hoped not.

Quite the contrary, she was comfortable with her life and the role her lovers played in it. When there were lovers, she thought. She didn't need the added distraction of being the topic of titillating conversations and rumors at gatherings that she and Tate would attend. She had never needed a woman in her life, and she certainly didn't intend to change because of someone like Tate.

When she pulled into her drive and approached the garage, a car she didn't recognize was parked in front of her front door. Instead of hitting the button to open the large door, she followed the curved drive and stopped directly in front of the vehicle. Her headlights illuminated the occupant.

Her heart jumped into her throat and her stomach lurched when she recognized Tate behind the wheel. *What is she doing here?* Victoria shifted into Park. *How does she know where I live? What does she want? For God's sake, it's almost midnight.* Those and a hundred other questions bounced through her brain in the time it took to shut off the engine and open the car door. Immediately Tate stepped out, her long legs silhouetted in Victoria's headlights.

"Tate?" Victoria asked, as if she hadn't recognized the woman who had occupied her thoughts for the past forty-five minutes.

"I hope I didn't scare you."

Victoria didn't answer the question, but posed one of her own. "How long have you been sitting out here?"

"About an hour. I was wondering who would show up first, you or the police, asking me if I was casing the joint."

"Are you?" Victoria asked, mimicking the humor of Tate's last statement. Tate walked toward her, and as she neared, Victoria was not at all surprised at the desire in her eyes. She knew hers probably mirrored the same but hoped they didn't.

"No, what I want is outside, not inside."

Tate's voice was husky, and it both frightened and thrilled Victoria. Tate stepped closer and Victoria smelled her perfume.

It was intoxicating. "You came to steal my pear tree?" Victoria propped herself against the hood of her car, making their eyes level.

"No, I came for you," Tate replied easily, stepping yet closer.

Victoria couldn't take her eyes off Tate's lips, which were now mere inches from her own. If she inched forward just a little she could taste them and end her torment. She clenched her fists to stop herself. "Do you intend to kidnap me so I don't land Braxton?"

"No."

Tate's warm breath caressed Victoria's lips and she could hardly breathe. "Then why are you here?" She wasn't sure she wanted to know the answer to the question but asked it anyway. If Tate put words to what was happening between them, then somehow it would become real. But if it just happened Victoria could wake up tomorrow and pretend it didn't. She was looking for a way out of consciously making a decision that could change the rest of her life.

"I think you know why I'm here."

"Are you trying to seduce me, thinking you'll get the upper hand with Braxton?" Why in God's name was she talking business when she had the hottest, most exciting woman waiting to kiss her, Victoria wondered as Tate's lips hovered over hers. This was the first time she had ever come close to crossing the line, and the longer Tate stood in front of her, the thinner the line became.

An instant before Tate kissed her, she said, "No, I'm here to seduce you because I want you."

Tate's lips were soft and light, causing an explosion of sensation. They were as warm as Victoria had imagined, tentatively exploring as if unsure what she would find. Tate had not stepped any closer, and Victoria had to arch her neck to maintain the contact.

After a few moments Tate murmured against her lips between

kisses, "I want to kiss you, taste you, run my hands over your body, feel your skin quiver under my fingertips. I want to hold you, explore you, go inside you."

At that point Victoria ignored her better judgment, recklessly leapt into the unknown, and pulled Tate to her. Wrapping her arms around Tate's neck she pressed against her hard body, deepening the kiss. Their tongues battled for control and she willingly surrendered to the sensations dominating her body. She grabbed Tate's short hair and pulled her closer, their lips crushing at their contact.

Tate was the first to break the kiss and Victoria immediately missed the connection. Tate's hands wandered up and down her back as her lips did the same on her neck. When she stopped and lightly nipped her neck just below her ear, Victoria's legs grew weak. She was breathing heavily, gasping for air. When Tate's hand closed around her breast she was jolted into realizing that her car headlights were illuminating everything that was happening. She fought down a giggle at the thought of her neighbors watching her make out at the front door.

As lost as Victoria was in the earthquake Tate was causing, she was together enough to know that this wasn't the place to make love. The back patio was out of sight of the prying eyes of neighbors and was a definite possibility, but her sense of propriety won out there too. This time Victoria broke the embrace and took two unsteady steps toward her front door. Her hand was shaking as she inserted the key into the lock. She quickly stepped inside and deactivated the alarm, then saw that Tate hadn't moved from where she left her.

This was the moment that Victoria had been dreading. The moment where she had to make a conscious decision and not use the excuse of *it just happened.* She never thought that things just happened, preferring to believe that people were always aware of what they were doing and could stop at any time. But with her body reacting to Tate as she stood there gazing at her, for the first time in her life, Victoria was helpless to say no.

CHAPTER FIFTEEN

It wasn't just because the interior of the house was dark that Tate allowed Victoria to lead the way. At this point, she would have let Victoria take her anywhere and do anything to her. She had originally come here intending to seduce Victoria. She knew she could, it would be almost too easy. She would spend the night with Victoria and get her out of her system so she could think clearly. If she could talk to her, really talk to her without the wall of Braxton between them, she could get her to see what Tate envisioned. It would be the ultimate in success, and she couldn't conceive that Victoria would tell her no.

But somewhere after the first touch of Victoria's lips, she lost all thought of business and control. And for once she didn't care. She had never been so consumed by a woman before. Tate was swept away by the taste of Victoria, the way her lips were tentative at first then effortlessly molded to hers. Neither of them spoke, and the plush carpet on the stairs muffled their footsteps. Tate's heart beat so loud it deafened her, and her head spun when she focused on Victoria's ass moving on the step above her.

Victoria released her hand as they entered the bedroom and continued across the room. She switched on the light beside the bed, splashing a soft warm glow over the room. Victoria hesitated and for a moment, Tate thought she would change her mind. When Victoria finally moved toward her, unbuttoning her blouse at the same time, Tate's knees went weak.

Victoria didn't stop until the lace of her bra peeked out from between the open buttons and their breasts touched. Victoria's hands dropped from her blouse to Tate's buckle while her eyes never left hers. Victoria's pupils dilated, passion flashing deep inside the blackness.

The clink of her belt and the pop of her pants' snap was the signal Tate needed to become a full-fledged participant. Her hands shook when she pulled Victoria's blouse off her shoulders. Unable to resist, she captured the lips waiting for her.

Victoria's hands roamed up and down her spine, pulling Tate's shirt out of her waistband. She took advantage of the full access to Tate's flesh and her hands quickly disappeared under the soft fabric. Tate needed to feel Victoria's breasts, but she slowly unhooked the blue bra that barely concealed what was underneath. Slowly, deliberately Tate slid the straps off Victoria's shoulders, all the while tracing the path with her fingers. She would never see Victoria's breasts for the first time again, and she wanted to savor the moment. Victoria's skin was soft and warm, and when the bra hit the floor Tate retraced its path.

Her hands were filled with the weight of Victoria's breasts, nipples hard against her palm. Victoria moaned and Tate needed to feel skin against skin. She withdrew her hands long enough to pull her own shirt over her head and gathered Victoria to her again. The sensation of Victoria's breasts against her was exquisite. Tate used Victoria's height to her advantage. Her erect nipples were almost level with her mouth, and she had only to bend slightly to capture one of them in her mouth.

Victoria leaned against her, wrapping her arms around her neck. When Tate teased the nipple with her tongue, Victoria grabbed her hair and pulled her mouth closer. After what she thought wasn't nearly long enough, she shifted her attention to Victoria's other breast for equal attention. She wasn't sure, but Tate thought she heard Victoria call her name.

"Hmm?"

"I have to lie down or we'll end up on the floor," Victoria said between gasps.

"My thoughts exactly." Tate dragged her mouth away from Victoria's breasts. She wanted to rip the remaining clothes from their bodies but for some reason gave in to the conflicting emotion of wanting to go slow, to draw out the experience. When she lowered Victoria to the bed, she knew she had made the right decision.

In spite of their height difference, Victoria fit perfectly under her. Tate returned to Victoria's lips, and then Victoria took charge, exploring her mouth and tongue with a thoroughness that almost sent Tate into oblivion. Tate was so overcome with desire that she almost forgot her purpose, which was to feel Victoria's naked body against hers.

The next thing Tate knew, almost every inch of their bodies was touching. Victoria had long legs but their torsos were almost exactly the same length. Victoria raised her body and slowly lowered it again until their nipples touched. The combination of hard arousal and soft flesh merged like yin and yang. Victoria arched against her, their pubes rocking against each other, expressing their desire.

Tate pulled away from Victoria's grasp, trailing kisses up and down her neck, stopping to pay particular attention to those areas where she discovered that Victoria was exceptionally sensitive. Each time she moaned or moved beneath her was a new experience in ecstasy for Tate. She had given countless women pleasure but none had excited her like Victoria was doing right now, and she welcomed Victoria's touch. Exploring a woman, making her cry out in passion was the foreplay Tate usually needed to climax. She was more into it for what she needed than for what the woman was getting. But with Victoria it wasn't like that. Not at all.

She wanted to please Victoria for the sheer pleasure of pleasing her. She wanted to kiss her senseless, taste every inch of her, feel her warmth, touch her deep inside. She could make love to her for hours and still not get enough.

Victoria, however, had other ideas. She used her long legs as leverage and flipped Tate onto her back, and when Victoria's thigh pressed against her and her mouth latched on to her nipple, Tate exploded. Lights flashed behind her eyelids and a roar slammed into her head. Wave after wave crashed over her and she couldn't catch her breath. The world seemed to fall away and only the strong arms wrapped around her supported her. One orgasm followed another as Victoria's hand replaced her leg, rubbing her clitoris in rhythm with her own thrusts.

Finally, Tate had to stop or risk death by overdose from the sensations cascading through her. She slid her hand down Victoria's arm, grasping her wrist loosely. She didn't have the strength to pull it away, but Victoria got the message and slowly withdrew her fingers from between her legs. Victoria held her close as the aftershock of her multiple orgasms settled.

The emotions threatening to spill out of Tate overwhelmed her. This was more than just physical release. It was something very different. She felt it deep inside. It touched her core and she didn't know what to do with it. Sex had always been more than just an enjoyable experience. She considered it as normal a need as food or water. But this was far from just sex, though Tate had no idea what it was.

"Wow," Victoria whispered into her neck. Tate found it difficult to breathe and chose to blame it on Victoria's body on top of her.

"That's one way to phrase it." Actually it was an understatement but Tate wasn't ready to admit it.

"I didn't realize you were that close." Victoria moved so the majority of her weight no longer pressed on top of Tate.

"Neither did I," Tate admitted, embarrassed by her lack of self-control. "It came out of nowhere, so to speak." She had to fight to maintain eye contact when Victoria looked at her.

"Well, you can come out of nowhere anytime," Victoria replied, lifting her eyebrows up and down a few times.

Suddenly feeling very uncomfortable and vulnerable, Tate shifted and quickly reversed their positions. This was where she felt most in control. On top, in charge. She was the aggressor and wasn't comfortable in any other position, which was what surprised her most about her recent orgasms. She was never able to climax with a woman on top of her like Victoria had been. She felt trapped and needed the woman either beside her using her hand or between her legs using her mouth. Even then more times than not lately she had to concentrate on what was happening in order to come.

Unwilling to deal with her troubling thoughts, Tate traversed the tall body beneath her. Victoria was uninhibited in her response to Tate's caresses. She moaned when Tate nibbled on her nipple, sighed when she kissed the small of her back, and thrust her hips toward any part of Tate that came even close to her clitoris.

Victoria's legs went on forever and Tate wrapped them around her neck for the sheer joy of the picture in her mind. Victoria grabbed the sheet in each hand as Tate finally settled her mouth on her. Tate pulled back when she sensed that Victoria was seconds away from coming. She was rewarded with another moan and Victoria rising to meet her mouth again.

"God, Tate, you're killing me," Victoria said softly.

Tate didn't reply, too focused on what she was doing with her mouth to bother to reply. Victoria tasted delicious and felt exquisite. She was soft and hard in all the right places. Tate ran the tip of her tongue over folds, peaks, and valleys, and dipped into warm wetness. The tension in Victoria increased as she moved her tongue in and out of her. Finally, after just a few plunges inside her Victoria grabbed her head, held it in place, and cried out.

❖

Victoria woke to the feel of an arm wrapped around her and a warm body pressed against her back. Tate breathed evenly onto her neck, and Victoria didn't move for fear of waking her. What had she done? For God's sake, what had she done? Images of the night before flooded her brain like water over a dam. Legs intertwined, hands, lips, mouths and tongues exploring every inch of her body while she delighted in Tate's young, firm flesh. Tate was an amazing, enthusiastic, and unrelenting lover. She demanded from Victoria as much as she gave, and when Victoria was certain she couldn't have another orgasm, Tate proved her wrong.

She tilted her head to look at the clock. It was just after seven and the sun was beginning to peek over the horizon. She could barely remember the last time she had woken with a woman in her bed. Even with Carole, when they had sex, one of them would get up and go home almost before their orgasm was over. She had thought it satisfying until last night with Tate.

What exactly was last night? They had sex, sure, by God did they ever. But why? What did it mean? What did it signify going forward? What were they supposed to do now? Were they supposed to sit across from each other at Braxton's meetings and act like it never happened? What did Tate expect from her? What did she expect from Tate? Would they do it again?

Tate pulled her closer and Victoria tensed, those and dozens of other questions bombarding her. She pushed them aside and tried to figure out how she could get out of bed without waking Tate. She didn't know what to say to her and knew it was chicken to slip out on her. Fuck, she thought. This was *her* house. It wasn't as if she could simply leave. Tate must have sensed her trepidation.

"Relax." Tate's voice was husky from sleep. "As much as I want a repeat of last night, give me a few minutes to wake up and then I'll leave."

Victoria didn't know what to do. It was childish to act this way. They were consenting adults, obviously attracted to each other. *No big deal. Happens all the time. Nothing to be embarrassed about. It's as natural as stars in the sky.* She was a mature woman. Oh, God, she was more than ten years older than Tate, she thought, wanting to crawl under the carpet. For crying out loud, she was the one who invited Tate in. She should be handling this better.

Not knowing what else to say, Victoria asked, "Would you like some coffee?" She could certainly use some. Maybe the influx of caffeine would jolt some sense into her.

"Only if someone besides you gets up, makes it, and brings it in." Tate snuggled closer, the tops of her thighs flush with the back of Victoria's legs. "I don't want you to go anywhere," Tate added, eliminating any doubt.

Victoria settled back into the warm embrace and tried to let her mind relax as well. Disjointed thoughts, accusations, recriminations, and doubt left little room to enjoy the sensation of being in Tate's arms. Why couldn't she just simply enjoy the morning after a night of fabulous sex with a very attractive woman? She certainly enjoyed it while it was happening. She couldn't help but finally smile.

Her body must have given off some other signal other than a smile because Tate asked, "What?"

"Nothing." Victoria admitted to herself that last night was the most intense experience of her life, but she refused to tell Tate. *Jeez, like Tate didn't already know.*

"You're amazing, Victoria," Tate commented, her voice a little more clear.

"Thanks. Right back at 'cha." Victoria couldn't help but chuckle over her reply. It sounded like they were complimenting each other over a game of tennis, not hour after hour of astounding sex.

Tate began to nibble the back of her neck, causing shivers to run down her spine. Victoria hadn't noticed when Tate had shifted her hand so that it cradled her breast, but her hard nipple was certainly aware of it. And speaking of hard nipples, Tate's were pressed against her back and left little to the imagination as to her level of arousal.

"You know, I'm not really a morning person," Tate whispered into her ear.

"But?" Victoria prodded. She knew where Tate was going with this, and even though a moment ago she had misgivings about the entire episode, she didn't want her to stop.

"But you make me want to wake up." Tate's hand left her breast and began to explore her stomach in tiny circles.

Victoria caught her breath when Tate's fingers drifted lower. She lay back into Tate, giving her more access to her body. "Does that mean you want coffee now?" Tate's wandering hand dipped between her legs and slipped easily inside her. Victoria barely stifled a moan of sheer pleasure at the contact. She was more than ready, and when Tate's fingers slid out, then back in again and repeated the movement, she gave in.

"No, I want you. *Again*," Tate said, as if it were a complete surprise.

Soon Victoria came again, this time in the soft pre-dawn light. The sun cast shadows over the wall that reminded her of waves softly rolling to the shore. Her climax was just the opposite—building from her toes, coursing to her center like a flame licking fuel. She cried out, reaching behind her to hold Tate closer. Together they rocked, Tate's fingers buried deep inside her, her pussy rubbing against Victoria's ass. Tate came after Victoria's third orgasm.

❖

When Victoria woke again, she was alone. The place where Tate had lain was cool to her touch, telling Victoria that she had left some time ago. She listened for the sound of the shower and, hearing nothing but silence, pushed the covers back and slid out of bed.

She had to grab the nightstand for balance, every muscle

in her legs making it very clear they had been used in ways they weren't accustomed to. She couldn't help but smile when she thought what her friends would say if they knew. She half wanted to say something, just to see their reaction and bask in their attention, but she had confessed to Tate she wasn't the type of woman to kiss and tell. Shit, until last night she didn't have anything *to* talk about.

Grabbing her robe from the hook in the closet, she quickly checked herself in the bathroom mirror. Her hair was a mess, but her eyes were clear and she didn't look any different after a night of sex. Returning to the bedroom she noticed that her clothes were neatly folded on the cedar chest and Tate's were conspicuously gone. She glanced up just as Tate walked in carrying two cups. The steam drifting from the top as well as the familiar aroma told her that Tate had found the coffeepot. She smiled at her shyly, her robe slipping off one shoulder.

Tate handed Victoria the cup and gave in to the temptation to kiss the bare flesh. Victoria shuddered under her lips. "I thought you could use this. I know I can. I hope you don't mind. I didn't have to snoop much. Everything was pretty much where I expected it to be." Tate couldn't believe she was rambling. She was nervous and didn't know why. She was never nervous the morning after. If she suspected the woman might become clingy or demanding, she always left before it ever had a chance to happen. With Victoria, she wanted to stay all day.

"No, not at all. It smells wonderful." Victoria took the cup in both hands.

Their fingers touched and a jolt of desire rocketed to Tate's crotch. She had to concentrate so she wouldn't drop her cup. "You were sleeping and I didn't want to wake you. You looked so peaceful and content." In fact, Tate had wanted to wake Victoria with soft kisses but satisfied herself with watching her sleep for a few minutes before she got up.

Victoria crossed to the bed and sat on the edge, drawing one leg under her. "At least I wasn't snoring."

"I never said that," Tate countered, enjoying the expression of horror that flashed across Victoria's face. She had to laugh. "Don't worry, you weren't snoring. As a matter of fact, you were so still I wasn't sure you were even breathing. Kind of threw me there for a minute until you moved."

"Sorry." Head averted, Victoria took a sip of her coffee.

Tate sat next to Victoria on the bed, slightly unnerved by the uncomfortable silence between them. A thousand thoughts were jumbled in her brain and she was trying to make sense of them. While she had watched Victoria sleep and contemplated the coffee dripping into the carafe, she realized everything felt right. The time they spent together, their getting to know one another in Brussels and Hong Kong, her nursing Victoria while she was sick in Phoenix were some of the most memorable experiences in her life. However, she couldn't dwell on them too long. She glanced at the clock on the bedside table.

"I hate to do this, but I've got to go."

"Okay," Victoria was quick to respond.

"No, really. It sounds like an excuse to get out of here but I have an appointment in an hour that I can't miss. I'm going to be late as it is." She did have an appointment with Clayton, one he demanded she attend in his office this morning. She would be late, but for the first time she didn't care.

"Sure, I understand."

Tate followed Victoria out of the bedroom and down the stairs. Her mind flashed back to the last time they were on the stairs together, heading in the opposite direction and intent on something altogether different. Leaving her cup on the counter, Tate hesitated, not quite sure what Victoria expected from her or what she expected from Victoria. When Victoria seemed equally uncertain, Tate stepped forward and placed a light kiss on her cheek.

"Thanks for inviting me in." Victoria flushed with embarrassment. She lifted Victoria's chin so she could look into her eyes. "You're a wonderful, exciting woman, Victoria, and I'd like to do this again." She saw the doubt creep into her eyes.

"Tate—"

"Just think about it. I'll talk to you in a few days." Tate placed a contained kiss on Victoria's lips. When Victoria's mouth immediately opened, Tate was barely able to restrain herself from picking up where they left off earlier that morning. She headed for the door before she convinced herself to stay.

Chapter Sixteen

Tate walked into her meeting with Clayton later that morning feeling smug. While she waited for him to end his phone conversation she redecorated his office in her mind to suit her tastes. The massive oak desk he currently had his feet on, the top scarred from the wear of his favorite shoes, would be the first thing to go. Though Clayton evidently sat behind the monstrosity to compensate for his small stature, it made him look ridiculous. She would lighten the décor with lots of chrome and sleek lines of modern furniture and accent pieces. The rattle of the phone receiver settling into the cradle drew her attention back to the present. Clayton was eyeing her with seeming annoyance.

"Well?"

"Drake will be out of the running before the end of the week." Her source's information and what she had gotten from Victoria's briefcase would not only harm Drake's attempts to acquire Braxton; it would cripple it and most likely cause the company to close. Joni had wanted to consummate their business transaction last night, but Tate's libido was focused on someone else. Joni went home frustrated but employed, while Tate went to Victoria's.

Since leaving Victoria's house Tate had spent most of her time figuring out exactly what to do with the time bomb Joni had handed her.

"Really? You sound pretty cocky."

At one time Tate would have thought that was a compliment. Now she considered it demeaning. "I know what I'm doing, Clayton."

"You'd better, Monroe. I told you I want Braxton and I won't stop until I get it." In no time, he was practically foaming at the mouth.

Tate stood, uncharacteristically unable to control her temper. She had always respected Clayton and his approach to business. It was often cutthroat, sometimes ruthless, and occasionally just this side of legal. And more often than not it was immoral. But she knew all that when she came to work for him years ago. That was why she specifically targeted him and his company for a position there. She wanted the success Clayton Sumner had attained, and if she had to copy his every move to get it, then so be it. That he couldn't see that even now was insulting.

"Jesus Christ, Clayton, I said I'd get it and I will. Stop treating me like I have shit for brains." Tate had never spoken to him like this and it caught both of them off guard. She was suddenly tired of fighting for everything, including the respect of the old man who was glaring at her. She thought she had earned it by now, but obviously she was mistaken. Not risking another outburst, she strode out of the office a little quicker than she had entered it.

Tate was still fuming an hour later, furious with herself for letting her emotions dominate her discussion with Clayton. *Calm* and *coolheaded* were the words she used to describe herself when it came to business. Calculating, cold, and heartless were what others called her. Her senses were overloaded after her night with Victoria, she rationalized. Yeah, that was it. She was groggy and exhausted from lack of sleep. She wasn't thinking clearly and let her mouth run before she engaged her brain. *Bullshit.*

No matter how sensible or logical her excuses sounded, Tate knew they were crap. She couldn't stop thinking of Victoria before *and* after she had had sex with her. Just when she thought she had Victoria figured out she surprised her. When she thought she knew what she was thinking, she would say something altogether different. When Tate expected a certain reaction, Victoria gave her just the opposite.

Early evening traffic in Atlanta was miserable as her cab crawled uptown to her favorite steakhouse. She'd earned it, she thought, and tapped her fingers impatiently on her thigh. She was still put out over her conversation with Clayton and needed to calm down before she did something stupid. *Like sleep with Victoria? How much more stupid could you get?* After she left Victoria she had gone back to her apartment to change for her meeting with Clayton. She barely had time to get her lust for Victoria back under control before she entered the old man's office.

She had fully intended to tell Clayton what she had learned about Drake that would destroy any chance they had of getting Braxton, but his attitude toward her squelched all desire to share her information. She would do it on her own, Clayton Sumner be damned. With the information she had dug up as well as what Joni had given her, Tate could bring Drake to its financial knees with one phone call. Drake was hemorrhaging money. All she needed was to drop a discreet bug in Victoria's investment banker's ear and it would be over. Drake's stock would tank, her money source would dry up, and Tate could sweep in and buy Braxton for substantially less than its real value. It was as simple as that. But Tate had an even better idea that had been dancing around in her head for a few days.

She looked up when the waiter brought the check, barely remembering that she had eaten dinner. Out of habit, and based on the itemized bill, she must have ordered the shrimp-and-steak combination. She licked her lips and tasted just a hint of garlic from the sautéed mushrooms.

Tate sipped the wine that remained in her glass. The restaurant was quiet and she gathered her scattered thoughts. Unfortunately she didn't know what to do with them. She had never experienced this sense of unease, almost like a constant state of anticipation. The deal for Braxton wasn't to blame, even though the logistics and negotiations were unusual. She could get Braxton, but was simply waiting until she made her move. She had been in this position more times than she could remember. She was born for this, had trained for this, had gloried in this. So what was going on?

She paid the check and walked out into the cool night. "What in the hell am I doing? I'm acting like a lovesick puppy, for God's sake," she said out loud. "Jesus, Monroe, get it together."

At that moment she realized Victoria was throwing her off-kilter. Victoria fascinated her and she was continually trying to figure her out. But it wasn't the business side that was causing her restlessness. It was the woman herself. Somewhere along the line she had fallen for Victoria Sosa and fallen hard.

Chapter Seventeen

Tate was seated at the table when Victoria arrived. She was surprised that she had been able to persuade Victoria to meet her for dinner, and when Victoria walked across the room, she was glad she had. She stood as Victoria approached, her pulse quickening in response to their night together. She knew every inch of her body—the way she felt, the way she smelled, the way she cried out her name. Tate took a deep breath to get her body back in control.

While she had waited for Victoria to arrive, Tate wondered what Victoria would do when they saw each other again. Would she kiss her hello, would she carry on a normal conversation as if they hadn't spent hours in the most intimate, compromising, and pleasurable positions? Would Victoria be able to look her in the eye? Tate didn't want to give her the chance to set the mood so she took her hand and kissed her lightly on the cheek. "I'm glad you could make it. You look beautiful."

Victoria had chosen a deep blue silk suit with a cream-colored turtleneck peeking out from under the jacket. A silver brooch of an abstract design winked at Tate from the left lapel.

"Thanks," Victoria replied, and sat down in the chair to Tate's left.

"Would you like something to drink?" Tate asked as the waiter headed their way. It was Saturday night and the restaurant was busy. She had pre-tipped the waiter to keep his attention focused on them this evening.

Victoria looked at her wineglass as if deciding whether to have a glass or not. "No, just water with lemon for me."

The thick carpet and oversize furniture muted the noise of the restaurant. They were tucked back into a corner that offered them more privacy than the other patrons. Tate had specifically requested this table when she called earlier and made reservations. What she had to say to Victoria required it.

After they placed their order Tate struggled for something to say. Her ability for small talk had always been minimal at best, but sitting next to Victoria after what they had done together two days ago made her mind mush. Was it only the day before yesterday? It felt like much longer.

She studied Victoria's profile. The candlelight flickering in the center of the table cast a soft glow on everything in the booth. Victoria didn't need any help to look beautiful. Her hair was up and her face, though slightly drawn, was still striking.

"You don't look very happy to be here," Tate said, commenting on the frown creasing Victoria's forehead.

Victoria finally looked at her and her scowl deepened. "I'm sorry. I'm not in the best of moods this evening. Lots on my mind..." Her explanation was weak.

"Anything you want to share?"

Victoria fiddled with her knife, seeming to think about the offer. "Maybe later."

Their food came and Tate was finally able to make conversation, but Victoria's answers to her questions were short and often didn't invite further exchange.

"Would you like to take a walk?" Tate decided to have the serious part of their discussion outside instead of at the table.

Victoria agreed, and within ten minutes Tate had paid the bill and they were walking down the almost-empty sidewalk.

"I have a proposition for you," Tate said, then wanted to pull her words back when she saw Victoria's frightened expression.

"No, not that kind of proposition," Tate replied quickly, finally laughing for the first time that evening. "Well, maybe later," she added, repeating Victoria's earlier comment, and grinned. "It's a business proposition."

This time Victoria's expression was wary.

"Now hear me out," Tate said. "I want Braxton. I don't need to tell you that, but what you don't know is why. If I get this deal, Clayton Sumner will hand over the reins of Sumner Enterprises to me. I'll control one the largest companies in the world. And I want you by my side." Tate hadn't prepared to say it quite that way, but what the hell. It was the truth.

"What?" Victoria stopped in the middle of the sidewalk.

Tate stood directly in front of Victoria and repeated her statement. "I want you beside me. Imagine it, Victoria, what we could do. There would be no stopping us, the money we could make, the businesses we could own, the empire we could build." Tate was excited at the prospect and didn't even try to hide it in her voice.

Victoria shook her head several times. "What?"

"Victoria, I'm going to get Braxton and then I'll bring in Drake as well, or what's left of it, and you can still run it if you want to. But you're better than that, Victoria. You could write your own ticket at Sumner. You and I will be on the cover of every major business magazine in the world." Tate fanned out her arms as if panning a billboard.

"Tate, I don't want—"

Tate took Victoria's hands in hers. "Victoria," she said calmly. "We're good together. We could be great if you'll give it half a chance. We could work together and be together. How more perfect can it be?"

Victoria pulled her hands away from Tate and stepped back. "I don't want to be with you, Tate, certainly not in business. You and I look at things very differently and there is no way—"

"Okay, we don't have to work together that closely. You can do your own thing at Sumner and I'll do mine." She was prepared to counter every argument Victoria threw at her. She would wear her down eventually.

"Tate, you don't understand." Victoria's voice rose. "I am not going into business with you nor will I be your lover."

"What?" It was Tate's turn to be confused.

"I have a company. I'm not looking to have another, particularly Sumner Enterprises, and especially not with you. I am working hard to get Drake back on its feet again, not sell it out for a quick buck and gobs of power. That's not who I am. And I'm also not looking to be a part of a power couple, as you phrased it. Been there, done that, and not interested in doing it again. I don't know where you ever got the idea that I'd be interested in Sumner. Clayton Sumner is a sleaze, and I wouldn't work for him if he offered me the last job on earth. I'd never even consider it."

Victoria's words stunned her. What had she just said? How had she misread her so badly? Did their night of sex cloud her mind to reality? She thought they were good together and, as she said, would be even better together.

"Look, Tate. That night was wonderful for me. I, I've never experienced anything like it, but it doesn't change who I am or what I want out of life. I want Drake to survive and grow. I want to be with a woman who treats me as her equal in life, not as a business partner. I have no desire to compete against a company for the attention of a woman. I won't do it. I don't care who she is," Victoria stated firmly.

Tate didn't know if she was simply stunned, embarrassed, humiliated, or all three. She wanted to lash out at Victoria for making her look like a fool. She wanted to crush her and her silly happily-ever-after dream. Anger burned inside her, and if a man hadn't bumped into her as he passed, she might have done something she would have regretted later. Instead she clenched her teeth.

"Don't flatter yourself, Victoria. Sex had nothing to do with it. That was all it was—sex. Nothing more." She drew a breath to try to calm her nerves. "Since you're such an independent woman, Victoria, I'm sure you can see yourself home," Tate managed to choke out before she spun on her heel and walked away.

Victoria moved from the middle of the sidewalk and sat down on a bench that circled a tall pine tree. *What in the fuck just happened?* She had agreed to meet Tate, intending to tell her that what went on between them would never occur again. But her plan seemed immaterial after the bombshell Tate had just dropped. What had she done to give Tate the impression she would be interested in being in business with her? Clayton Sumner was a shark and his company the feeding pool. As soon as she learned of Tate's involvement in the Braxton deal she did her research on Sumner Enterprises and questioned their business ethics and their integrity.

She didn't think Tate was the kind of woman who believed that simply because Victoria had fallen into bed with her, she would fall into anything else with her. It was just sex, for God's sake. Tate had even said so herself. It wasn't as if they were in love. They hardly knew each other. Sure, they had spent three weeks together, often sixteen hours a day, but that was business, not a relationship.

She definitely wasn't interested in being a power couple. That's what happened with Melissa, and she would never agree to such a relationship again. *Power* wasn't a word she wanted associated with her professional life and certainly not her personal one.

After she tipped the valet and slid into the driver's seat of her car, she drove home like a robot and held her breath as she pulled into her driveway. She didn't expect to see Tate's car but was still more than a little relieved when the only thing in front of her house was the soft light from the porch.

She fixed a tall glass of scotch, took off her jacket, and dropped onto the sofa. Kicking her shoes off, she extended her legs until they lay on top of the coffee table. She lolled her head back and wondered how her world had gotten so off-kilter so fast. One minute she was a successful CEO and the next she was asked to ditch her company and run off to be on the cover of *Forbes* with her young lesbian lover. Was this what her life had become? If she kept it up she could be on *The Jerry Springer Show* and flaunt her low-class existence for the entire world to see. She was better than that and she knew it.

Chapter Eighteen

Tate was everywhere. In her dreams, her thoughts, even with her in the shower, metaphorically, of course. Victoria had refilled her glass four times before she went to bed last night, and her head was barking at her for doing so. Slowly she sipped her coffee and ate a piece of toast as the fog cleared from her brain. As it did, the one thing that became clear was that she felt more for Tate than she thought she did.

She had known she was curiously attracted to her the moment they ran into each other in the lobby of the Braxton building, but she had tossed her reaction off as simply that—a natural attraction to a beautiful woman. She attributed her awareness of Tate to their constant togetherness forced on them by Braxton. Who couldn't help but be aware of a business adversary sitting across the table and beside her all day? Especially one as alluring as Tate. She told herself she was listening to the questions Tate asked instead of the sound of her voice. She convinced herself that she was watching what Tate was looking at during their tours and not the shape of her mouth or the color of her eyes.

Who was she kidding? There was more to it than that and after that night they were together, she could no longer deny it. She had to face it, put it in its proper perspective, and move on. She was in no position to get involved with Tate personally and certainly not professionally. But damn if she didn't make her feel things she hadn't felt in a long time, if ever.

Tate grabbed life with both hands and lived it. She was aggressive without being domineering and rarely, Victoria guessed, took no for an answer. It wasn't just the fact that she was younger, although that was probably some of it. Tate had a maturity level that belied her age. The sex was the best she had ever had but certainly not enough for an enduring relationship. It was the total package that interested Victoria.

Victoria threw a load of clothes in the wash, grabbed a bottle of water, and opened the French doors that led out to her patio. She settled into one of the lounge chairs and stretched her legs out in front of her again. She relived the past few months mentally, but her body reminded her of the last few days. She really didn't know that much about Tate other than what she had gleaned from the Internet and a few well-placed sources. But what was indisputable was that Tate made her feel alive again. What was she going to do about it?

❖

"Tate, Victoria Sosa is here to see you."

Tate froze at the name of the woman her administrative assistant said was waiting in her outer office. *Victoria? Here to see me? What does she want? Probably to tell me again in no uncertain terms that she wants nothing to do with me,* Tate thought in the second it took her to find her voice. She didn't want to see Victoria. One humiliation was enough; she didn't want or need another.

"She said it's important."

"I'm sure it is," Tate muttered under her breath. "Show her in, and if she's not out of here in ten minutes, come in and make some excuse for me." Tate braced herself.

She was in no way prepared for her reaction when Victoria walked through the door. She wore a navy jacket over tan slacks and a pale blue shirt. Her hair was pulled back, and Tate realized she really liked it that way. Her gaze was steady as she strode into her office with purpose.

"Victoria, I didn't expect to see you here." Tate greeted the woman who had rocked her world. When she hadn't heard from Victoria in a week after her disastrous proposition, she thought Victoria was lost to her forever. She indicated for Victoria to sit in one of the chairs in front of her desk. "What can I do for you?" By now Tate was intrigued by what Victoria had to say. Had she reconsidered Tate's proposal from that night? Was she here to take her rightful place next to Tate on this throne? She doubted it. Tate sat back in her chair, waiting impatiently for Victoria to reveal why she was here.

"It's about Braxton."

"I'm sure it is," Tate said, not even trying to hide her sarcasm.

"Tate, please."

"Please? Please what, Victoria?" Tate moved out from behind her desk. "Please let me have Braxton? Please don't take Drake away from me? Please don't put hundreds of people out of work?" She stared at Victoria, suddenly furious. She had embarrassed and humiliated herself because she had fallen for this woman, and she wasn't about to make that mistake again. She reverted to what she knew best, sarcasm and aggression. Victoria looked as though she had been struck, but then her face filled with anger.

"Did you take a class to learn how to be a bitch or does it just come naturally?" Victoria stood and Tate felt as if she were towering over her—not just by inches.

"Very good, Victoria," Tate replied, impressed by her wicked stab. "I didn't think you had it in you."

"I don't. You just bring out the best in me."

Tate couldn't help but remember their night together and found that her statement was true. She said as much, fully intending to leverage what she knew about Victoria to her advantage. "Yes, Victoria, I did bring out the best in you." She knew she was successful when Victoria recognized the reference and her eyes blazed.

"I don't even know why I bothered."

She stood and Tate watched her back as she calmly walked out.

❖

Victoria walked across the street oblivious to the people spilling over the white lines of the crosswalk. She entered a generic coffee shop, ordered a large decaf, and sat at the counter facing the street. It was just after five and people were scurrying from their offices to dates or running errands before their long commute home. She loved the energy of the city—the pulse of the traffic, the solid beat of commerce, of business being conducted every day. But today everything was a blur.

What was she thinking by trying to talk to Tate? Did she really believe they would sit down and chat about her proposition over coffee? That they would talk through the misperception between them and everything would be like it was before? Before what? Before they spent hours exploring each other's bodies? Before they cried out in ecstasy under each other's caresses? Her hands shook at the thought.

She was surprised when Tate exited her building and hailed a cab. Victoria hadn't had the opportunity to notice much about how Tate looked. Her body was doing all the talking when she initially saw her. Tate was wearing dark trousers with a blistering white shirt tucked in at the waist. Her belt buckle was small but glinted in the sun. She had put sunglasses on the instant she stepped out from the revolving door, and Victoria remembered how she always wore them when they were outside. The light breeze ruffled her hair as she waited impatiently on the curb, and Victoria's fingers tingled at the memory of how soft it was.

Victoria remembered everything about Tate. Every minute they spent together, every conversation, every touch. She had fallen for her and couldn't figure out why. What was it about her that made her pulse race at just at the thought of her? Made her heart pound when they were together? Made her want to be reckless and irresponsible and simply be with Tate?

A cab finally stopped and Tate slipped into the back. She was talking on her cell phone, one hand stabbing the air as the door closed. The cab took off and made a quick illegal U-turn and drove right in front of where she was sitting. For an instant, their eyes met before the cab was halfway down the street, turning right at the first corner. Victoria was angry, hurt, and suddenly very lonely.

Chapter Nineteen

Victoria dressed carefully. She was wearing what she called her don't-fuck-with-me suit, a classic Armani custom-tailored to her. The pleats on the jade green trousers still fell perfectly off her slim hips and creased just at the top of her shoes. The jacket was collarless with subdued brass buttons up to the neck. She left the jacket open, wearing a pearl white blouse underneath. She felt strong and powerful when she wore this outfit, and she needed everything she had to get through the meeting with Braxton's board of directors. Victoria was the first to complete the final step in this bizarre process. She had thirty minutes to present her business case as to why Braxton should sell to her company. She had been preparing it for four weeks, and the brisk Atlanta November morning invigorated her.

She was confident in her presentation but a bit jumpy worrying if she would see Tate today. She hadn't slept much last night, finally getting out of bed just after five. She ate a light breakfast and drank only two cups of coffee before she headed to her car to make the trek across town. The last thing she needed was to be late due to traffic, parking, or the multitude of other things that could delay her arrival.

Seventy-two hours later she was standing in front of her own board of directors. "Ladies and gentlemen, thank you for coming on such short notice." When she looked around the room and saw expectant faces, her stomach dropped farther than it already had. "Braxton didn't select us." She had rehearsed how she would break the news but found no way other than to be straightforward.

Murmurs and profanities drifted around the room. She spent the next quarter of an hour passing on the reasons Braxton had given for their selection. It was all about money. Pure and simple economics. "I'm sorry. I know you were counting on me."

"And you failed." Edward Hamacher said what she herself had been thinking but with much more venom in his voice.

"Edward, don't be so harsh," one of the other board members scolded in her defense.

"Well, she did. She said she would get it and she didn't. What are we supposed to say? Oops, good try, Victoria, better luck next time? This is the big leagues, folks. She didn't deliver what was needed." His face was red and his breathing fast.

Victoria swallowed. "Edward is right. It was my job to get Braxton and I didn't. I am responsible." Victoria looked every board member in the eye as she spoke. She knew what this meant. Now she would have to reverse roles and try to sell Drake. If they didn't find a buyer, they would be on the auction block.

She trudged down the hall to her office. The board had asked her to leave while they went into executive session.

She was sitting behind her desk when Edward Hamacher entered. He wore the same angry scowl he had in the board room.

"You're finished, Victoria," he growled.

"What?" Victoria wasn't certain she heard him correctly.

"You heard me, you're out. The board has lost confidence in you and we're making a change. You will receive the severance that's stipulated in your contract and we will prepare a press release to go out tomorrow morning. Robert will be named interim CEO." He was practically gleaming.

Victoria's heart thudded. Her ears began to ring, and she put a hand on her desk to keep from swaying. *Fired?* There wasn't much she could say. She understood the board's position. She had fallen short on a major goal, one the company desperately needed for its survival. If one of her staff had failed like this, she would fire them too. But it didn't make sense for Robert to be in charge. The head legal guy usually didn't know how to run a business. Victoria wanted to say as much, but there wasn't anything she *could* say. Hamacher filled the silence.

"You grossly miscalculated, Victoria. Maybe if you had fucked Braxton instead of your little dyke girlfriend you'd still have a job."

His comment and the hatred in his voice stunned Victoria. Was that what he thought of her? Was that what he thought she would do for this business? If she were a man, would he expect the same? Her heart lurched at his reference to Tate. She fought to maintain control and not show any outward sign that he had hit a nerve.

"Edward, I think you'd better—"

"Don't you dare tell me what I should and shouldn't do. You are fired. I suggest you leave now. Someone will pack up your things and send them to your house."

Victoria stood, and as much as he obviously tried not to, Edward leaned back just enough to tell her that she intimidated him. "Edward, I deserve more respect than this."

"You don't deserve shit." He was fuming, the spittle on his lips threatening to fly into her face. "You're getting far more than you deserve. You had better leave before I decide to tell the board all about your little rendezvous with our main competitor for this deal. What will the board think when they find out you've been sleeping with Tate Monroe?"

Victoria suddenly found it ironic that people always referred to sex as "sleeping with someone" when very little sleeping actually occurred. That was certainly the case with her and Tate. She fought down a wave of hysteria that threatened to bubble into laughter. She had never been questioned about her morals or integrity, and now at the biggest moment in her life she was faced with the ugliness of what she had done.

❖

Victoria hung up the phone and reached for her drink. The ice had melted while she talked with Claire, and as a result the scotch had lost of some its kick as it slid down her parched throat. She had been on the phone with every member of her staff the entire evening. One after another she called them and broke the news that Drake was not selected and she had been removed as CEO. They were all stunned and had offered their assistance, Claire even offering to leave with her in a show of support. Victoria had spent the last hour trying to talk her out of it. She wasn't sure if she succeeded.

What did she do now? She didn't need to find a job right away but she needed to work. Not just for the income but for herself, her sense of self-worth. But where? The satisfaction she got out of her work at Drake transcended anything she could have imagined. She was contributing to something bigger than herself. Drake wasn't just a company making money for its shareholders. Drake saved the lives of people every day.

She had been working at one job or another for over thirty years without a break and realized she was tired. Tired of fighting—with Hamacher, for Drake's survival, her feelings for Tate. Two out of the three were taken care of, but the remaining one was a doozie.

Tate's proposition had stunned her. Had she misread their relationship so badly? She had thought Tate felt something for her. It was in her touch, her caress, the soft whispers in the darkness. But she had been wrong, so wrong.

What was she thinking? That Tate had harbored more than lust? She was young, vibrant, and on the fast track. They didn't run in the same social circles, certainly not in the same business circles. They had little in common, if anything, other than business. Now they didn't even have that.

Tate had won. She was sitting in the winner's circle and

with it would receive the culmination of her dreams. Victoria was sitting alone on her couch, her dream in tatters.

❖

"Here's to the new CEO of Sumner Enterprises." Clayton tapped his champagne glass against Tate's and swallowed its contents greedily. "I didn't think you could do it, Monroe, I really didn't think you could do it."

Tate cringed at her boss's verbal opinion of her. He had always jabbed at her like this, and she wondered why all of a sudden it bothered her. She bit her tongue to keep from saying as much.

"What's the first thing you're going to do, Monroe? Buy a flashy new car with that big fat raise I just gave you? Buy a beach house in the Bahamas and get yourself a little housegirl?" He chuckled at his own sense of humor.

"Redecorate my new office," she said lightly so as not to offend, but she was definitely serious. She was rewarded with Clayton's loud laugh.

"That's my girl, go for the bling. You deserve to look good. Nobody will take you seriously if you don't. It's not how much you have, it's what you do with it, Monroe. Intimidation is how this game is played. The one with the most toys always wins in the end."

And you have plenty, Tate thought. For some reason her success didn't have the sweet smell she expected it to have. She thought she would feel on top of the world. That she would feel like she owned the world. Instead she felt almost empty. Here she was, thirty-three years old, the CEO of a major multinational company, worth gobs of money, and she was sitting in a bar with a sixty-eight-year-old man. She should be celebrating with her friends or a lover, buying drinks for the house and basking in the compliments and accolades of her friends.

But she didn't have friends, she had business acquaintances.

They would give her accolades on another successful acquisition and want to know all the sneaky details. She had been there and done that many times. But this time was different. For the first time she clearly saw what Clayton was. He was an old man with a chip on his shoulder, thrice divorced, and a sloppy drunk. She didn't want to be him.

CHAPTER TWENTY

Tate wandered around her office, the sun casting shadows in the dimming afternoon light. It had been eight months since she claimed her place as the head of Sumner Enterprises at the first of the year, and her portfolio was larger than ever, as was her bank account. But something was missing. The thrill she anticipated wasn't there. The power she knew she would feel was absent. She had ascended to the pinnacle of her career and it wasn't at all what she had expected. In meetings she was revered, respected, and oftentimes even feared. She could have practically anything she wanted with the push of a button, but she was empty inside.

A few weeks after Clayton moved to Tahiti, Tate prowled around her living room, restless. She had plenty to do if it involved work, but for the first time in her life she wasn't interested in work. She scrolled through her address book and with some disappointment found that of the hundreds of names, not one of them was someone she could call to simply hang out with.

What had she done with her free time before she got this job? Who did she go out with? Where did she go? Did she work seven days a week, day and night? She must have. Why didn't she have a single friend? There were names of dozens of lovers but none that she had shared more than a dinner, a bottle of wine or two, and a good romp in the sheets with. As far back as she could remember all she could see was school, work, more school, her job with Clayton, meetings, secret information, and more meetings. What had she become?

She thought of Victoria more and more lately, as the excitement of her new job waned. She had been replaced at Drake, which had just declared bankruptcy. Tate had Googled her name several times but never found any information more recent than her position at the pharmaceutical company. Where was she and what she was doing?

In the middle of a workday last week, Tate had driven by Victoria's house and hoped she was outside so she could catch a glimpse of her but prayed she wasn't out of sheer embarrassment at her actions. She was thinking about her now, her fingers twitching to pick up the phone and call her. But what in hell would she say? "Hey, Victoria, wanna grab a bite?" Shit, she probably would take a bite of her ass instead. And speaking of bites on the ass, Tate wasn't accustomed to her body reacting the way it did when she thought of her. A shiver darted down her spine and her heart beat a little faster, occasionally skipping a beat or two. And invariably other parts of her body tingled as well.

She had no interest in other women, much to the chagrin of those who were interested in her for the power or money she now had. Joni Roseville, the woman who had approached her in the bar and given her much-needed information on Drake, had stopped by her office several times when Tate was working late. The times she invited Tate for a drink, the look in her eyes carried more than a simple invitation for a nightcap. Tate always declined.

It was Victoria she wanted. Plain and simple, but nothing was plain and simple anymore. She missed the challenge of Victoria's mind, the way she studied a problem, her professionalism, her grace, and all the other little things that made her who she was. She was an astute businesswoman with an aptitude for analyzing every fact and synthesizing it in a sentence or two. She could ask the hard questions but wasn't afraid to heap praise on those who deserved it. She respected everyone and, most importantly, she respected herself.

Tate sighed, realizing how much it must have cost Victoria to get involved with her. What was she talking about? They weren't *involved*, they had sex. It wasn't a relationship, or an affair. Hell, it was barely even a fling. But it had meant something to Tate, and she realized it now. Victoria meant something to her. She had learned from her as well. She learned how to be a better person, a better businesswoman, without the hard edges and hard core.

If she walked away from Sumner Enterprises her career would be over. Old man Sumner had made it very clear that this was her ticket. He had punched it for the next leg of the journey and he could just as easily kick her off the bus. Tate knew Clayton would go ballistic. For some reason he was still adamant about Braxton, almost to the point of being irrational. Even though he had retired and usually left her alone, just this morning he had called and demanded to know if she had dismantled and sold off all the pieces of Braxton. Tate had made the appropriate noises and he went away satisfied. She didn't think she could pull it off again. For the first time in more years than she could remember, she wasn't sure she even wanted to.

❖

"Come in," Victoria called to the person knocking on her door. The individual walked in and within four steps was standing in front of her desk. At Drake, it would have taken at least fifteen.

"Yes, Sidney?" Victoria watched as the young woman fidgeted.

"Excuse me, Ms. Sosa, but you said to come to you if I had a question?"

Victoria smiled to put the young woman at ease and motioned

to the chair. "Of course, Sidney, sit down. How many times have I asked you to call me Victoria?" When the woman didn't reply she said, "What's up?"

Victoria had been at the Jackson Heights Center for just over a year. The non-profit rehabilitation center specialized in brain and spinal-cord injuries and was recently listed as one of the top healthcare centers in the state. She loved working here, especially knowing that she helped others make a difference in the lives of men, women, and children every day. At Drake she was too far removed from the day-to-day activities to see any real results. Here at the center, she shared in the residents' accomplishments even if they were as simple as picking up a potato chip without crushing it. Nothing was simple for these people.

The husband of an acquaintance had given her the lead on the job. Jackson Heights needed a new administrator, one with business experience who could fine-tune the operation into the best it could be. Victoria had never worked in this capacity, but her experience at Drake and her natural ability to interact with people and put them at ease got her the job. She was making a fraction of what she had before, but money wasn't what this job was all about. The grind of corporate America hadn't allowed much time for herself, but her new role did. She had started training for the Atlanta marathon in the fall and just this morning had run ten miles in the cool Atlanta spring morning.

Twenty minutes after the case worker left her office, another knock on her door made Victoria look up from the financial report she was reading. Her heart stopped and her mouth suddenly became very dry. Tate stood in her doorway.

She was wearing a red sweater over worn blue jeans and scuffed boots. Her hair was a little shorter and she looked wonderful. Tate's occupation of her brain had lessened a little, the new job needing more and more of the space. But at night, when her head crushed the pillow, everything flooded back.

"I hope I'm not disturbing you."

Victoria was almost too stunned to speak. Tate was the last

person she expected to see in her office but when she saw her casually supporting the doorjamb, Victoria finally admitted she was the only one she wanted to see.

"No, not at all," Victoria managed to say, her throat tight with emotion.

"Your assistant wasn't at her desk."

Victoria couldn't help but chuckle. "I don't have one. I share her with three other people." This was another major difference from her position at Drake. Tate stayed where she was but glanced around the tiny office. Victoria watched as she took in the plain décor. The expensive rug, the paintings on the walls, the mahogany furniture were gone. In their place were a few straight-backed chairs and two battered file cabinets. Four old paperbacks propped up the right rear corner of her desk, its leg missing. The thing that stunned Victoria was the expression on Tate's face as she took in her surroundings.

"This looks more like you," Tate said.

"Really?" Victoria wanted her to continue but didn't know how to ask.

Tate solved the problem by walking over to the bookcase and taking a small clay figurine off the shelf. It was a gift from one of the residents who had painstakingly made it in one of his rehab sessions, and it meant more to Victoria than any award she ever received.

"Yes, more relaxed, down-to-earth, comfortable."

"You wouldn't know that by the young woman who left here earlier. She was so nervous she made me nervous," Victoria replied. *Kind of like you're making me now.* Tate hadn't looked at her since entering her office, and Victoria couldn't stop staring at her. She remembered the feel of Tate's legs wrapped around her, the way the muscles in her back tightened when she ran her fingernails across them, the way Tate trembled in her arms. Tate chose that moment to turn around and their eyes met. The fire of something crossed her eyes before she blinked it away. What was it?

"May I sit down?" Tate motioned to a chair.

"Yes, of course, I'm sorry." Victoria sat in the chair adjacent to Tate. "Can I get you anything?"

"No, thanks, I'm fine." Tate fidgeted. "How have you been?"

The sound of Tate's voice drifted across the small space and into her ears. It was as refreshing as cool water on a hot day. She missed it and wanted to hear it again. "I'm fine. How about you?"

"I'm doing all right."

"I've been reading good things about you." Actually Victoria had gobbled up everything she could get her hands on about Tate. In the *Atlanta Business Journal* she saw the picture of her standing next to Clayton that accompanied the piece about the change of control at Sumner Enterprises. Every article she read detailed her rise to power and indicated that Tate was living her dream. She had finally broken the habit of Googling her name at least once a week.

"Not lately." Tate scoffed.

"What do you mean?" Victoria had been particularly busy these past few months getting ready for a fundraiser, which their major benefactors would attend.

Tate looked her straight in the eyes. "I've left Sumner," she said quietly but clearly.

Victoria wasn't sure she heard her correctly. Why would she leave after getting what she had worked so hard for? She asked as much.

"Because you weren't there to share it with me."

This time Victoria was too shocked to speak.

"I've missed you, Victoria. I know I messed everything up when I asked you to join me at Sumner. I was stupid. At the time I didn't know my butt from an oil well. All I knew was that I had to get to the top. It's all I had ever dreamed of and worked for. I didn't know any different."

Victoria found her voice. "What's changed?"

"Me. I'm a different person, Victoria. You made me a different person." This time Tate laughed. "I quit Sumner four months ago. It wasn't what I thought it would be and wasn't what I wanted. Now I own a house, push the lawnmower around my backyard, and have a dog named Merger. But you know what? I'm happy, really happy for the first time in my life. I'm happy with myself and who I am, not what I'm trying to be. Victoria, being with you made me this way."

"Tate—"

"Wait. Hear me out, please," she added, as if afraid Victoria would send her away. "I learned everything I now know from you. You've shown me things I never would have seen before, never had the opportunity to see. I was stupid, arrogant, calculating, and downright mean. If I could apologize to everyone I was ugly to I'd do it, but I can't. What I can do is thank you for coming into my life. Without you I'd still be that money-grabbing, cruel bitch that gobbled up companies and spat them out like a bad taste in my mouth. As I keep trying to say, I'm a different person, Victoria."

Tate hesitated before continuing. She took Victoria's hands. "But what's not different is how I feel about you. This time I know what to do about it. I love you, Victoria. I love everything about you. Your wit, your charm, the way you smile at someone when they're talking to you. The way your eyes light up when you're excited. Your determination, your guts, your perseverance. Your integrity. The way you kick my ass. I love you. I miss you. I miss being with you. I miss having you in the same room or knowing you're in the next room, or down the hall. For God's sake, Victoria, I have a white picket fence around my front yard!"

Victoria was stunned. What had Tate said? She quit Sumner, grew up, and fell in love with her? Did she hear all that correctly? She thought she had lost her somewhere around the part about her being a money-grabbing bitch until the *I love you* part came in. She heard every word of that. She hoped she knew what it meant. She prayed she didn't read more into the house with the white picket fence and the dog than was meant to be.

"I don't know what to say."

"What do you want to say?"

Victoria studied Tate. She had come here, more than a year after the event that tore them apart, and was sitting across from her a changed woman, declaring her love. The Tate she knew would never have admitted to any weakness, let alone bare it all at the risk of ridicule. She had changed and Victoria liked the new her. Even more than she did the old Tate. If Tate could expose herself this way, so could she. She smiled and tightened her grip on Tate's hand.

"You're very brave to come here, Tate. I could have kicked your sorry ass to the curb, called the cops, or any number of other things. But you came anyway. I admire you for that. I will admit I'm still a bit shocked that you're here."

In the past year Victoria had often dreamed of what she would say to Tate if she ever saw her again. Her feelings hadn't changed, but she had been able to put them in the proper perspective. They had been thrown together in a difficult situation for both of them, and they reacted as only they knew how. What had surprised Victoria was that at the most critical juncture of her life she had fallen in love with her polar opposite, the exciting woman sitting in front of her now.

She had done a lot of soul-searching since that fateful day when she was fired. She had taken the time to find herself—who she was, not who everybody wanted and expected her to be. For the first time in a long time she was comfortable with who she was, what she was doing, and what she wanted out of life. She refused to let it slip through her fingers. She hesitated, then plunged on.

"Because I've dreamed of it so often, I'm not sure you're really here. I've missed you too, more than I knew until the moment I saw you propped against my door with your cocky attitude and your fabulous body. I never imagined someone like you would be interested in me. Now wait." She put her free hand up to silence Tate's rebuttal. "You said yours, now it's my turn. You're at least ten years younger than me, more than that in many ways. You live life in the fast lane. I can't remember the last time I was even *near* the fast lane, let alone in it. You're very different from anyone I've ever known, and you scare me. But you excite me as well. You make me come alive. I see more, hear more, experience more when I'm with you. And I feel more. I didn't realize I'd been living under a cloud until you walked in. I love you, Tate Monroe. God help me, but I do."

Victoria realized her words must have come from the heart because she had no idea what would cross her lips until they were out. And she didn't regret a one of them.

"Wow," Tate said, shaking her head. "If I'd have known this would be your reaction, I'd have come months ago."

"We wouldn't have been ready for each other," Victoria said honestly. "At least I wouldn't have. I would have thrown you under the first bus that came along." She laughed. It felt good to laugh again.

"So what do we do now?" Tate asked.

"Do you really have a white picket fence around your house?"

"Absolutely. The minute I saw it I thought of you and had to have it. I heard what you said, Victoria, about not wanting to be a power couple. Maybe not at the time, but it's coming through loud and clear now. I don't want that either."

"What do you want, Tate?" Victoria needed the words to come out of her mouth. There could be no misconceptions over this.

"I want you in my life. In my house, in our house. Maybe even have a few kids together. I want to fight over the toothpaste, make up over a glass of wine, and hold you in my arms every night. I want to grow old with you, Victoria."

Victoria's heart swelled and she was afraid it might burst.

Just a few minutes ago she thought she was happy, but that was nothing compared to what she was feeling now. She could very easily echo every word back to Tate with the same emotion and sincerity that Tate emitted. Because it was true. She wanted to be with her for the rest of her life, however exciting and scary it might be. She stood and pulled Tate into her arms.

"Okay. Let's give it a try." And she kissed her.

About the Author

Julie Cannon is a native of Phoenix, Arizona, where she lives with her partner Laura and their two children. Julie's day job is in Corporate America and her nights are spent bringing to life the stories that bounce around in her head throughout the day. When not writing, Julie and Laura spend their time camping and lounging around the pool with their kids.

Julie is the author of five romances published by Bold Strokes Books: *Come and Get Me*, *Heart 2 Heart*, *Heartland*, *Uncharted Passage*, *Just Business*, and the upcoming *Descent*. She has short story selections in *Erotic Interludes 4: Extreme Passions*, *Erotic Interludes 5: Road Games*, *Romantic Interludes 1: Discovery*, *Romantic Interludes 2: Secrets*.

Visit Julie at www.juliecannon.com.

Books Available From Bold Strokes Books

Power Play by Julie Cannon. Businesswomen Tate Monroe and Victoria Sosa are at odds in the boardroom, but not in the bedroom. (978-1-60282-125-5)

The Remarkable Journey of Miss Tranby Quirke by Elizabeth Ridley. When love enters Tranby's life in the form of a beautiful nineteen-year-old student, Lysette McDonald, she embarks on the most remarkable journey of all. (978-1-60282-126-2)

Returning Tides by Radclyffe. Insurance investigator Ashley Walker faces more than a dangerous opponent when she returns to the town, and the woman, she left behind. (978-1-60282-123-1)

Veritas by Anne Laughlin. When the hallowed halls of academia become the stage for murder, newly appointed Dean Beth Ellis's search for the truth leads her to unexpected discoveries about her own heart. (978-1-60282-124-8)

The Pleasure Planner by Larkin Rose. Pleasure purveyor Bree Hendricks treats love like a commodity until Logan Delaney makes Bree the client in her own game. (978-1-60282-121-7)

everafter by Nell Stark and Trinity Tam. Valentine Darrow is bitten by a vampire on her way to propose to her lover Alexa Newland, and their lives and love are placed in mortal jeopardy. (978-1-60282-119-4)

Summer Winds by Andrews & Austin. When Maggie Turner hires a ranch hand to help work her thousand acres, she never expects to be attracted to the very young, very female Cash Tate. (978-1-60282-120-0)

Beggar of Love by Lee Lynch. Jefferson is the lover every woman wants to be—or to have. A revealing saga of lesbian sexuality. (978-1-60282-122-4)

The Seduction of Moxie by Colette Moody. When 1930s Broadway actress Violet London meets speakeasy singer Moxie Valette, she is instantly attracted and her Hollywood trip takes an unexpected turn. (978-1-60282-114-9)

Goldenseal by Gill McKnight. When Amy Fortune returns to her childhood home, she discovers something sinister in the air—but is former lover Leone Garoul stalking her or protecting her? (978-1-60282-115-6)

Romantic Interludes 2: Secrets edited by Radclyffe and Stacia Seaman. An anthology of sensual lesbian love stories: passion, surprises, and secret desires. (978-1-60282-116-3)

Femme Noir by Clara Nipper. Nora Delaney meets her match in Max Abbott, a sex-crazed dame who may or may not have the information Nora needs to solve a murder—but can she contain her lust for Max long enough to find out? (978-1-60282-117-0)

The Reluctant Daughter by Lesléa Newman. Heartwarming, heartbreaking, and ultimately triumphant—the story every daughter recognizes of the lifelong struggle for our mothers to really see us. (978-1-60282-118-7)

Erosistible by Gill McKnight. When Win Martin arrives at a luxurious Greek hotel for a much-anticipated week of sun and sex with her new girlfriend, she is stunned to find her ex-girlfriend, Benny, is the proprietor. Aeros Ebook. (978-1-60282-134-7)

Looking Glass Lives by Felice Picano. Cousins Roger and Alistair become lifelong friends and discover their sexuality amidst the backdrop of twentieth-century gay culture. (978-1-60282-089-0)

Breaking the Ice by Kim Baldwin. Nothing is easy about life above the Arctic Circle—except, perhaps, falling in love. At least that's what pilot Bryson Faulkner hopes when she meets Karla Edwards. (978-1-60282-087-6)

It Should Be a Crime by Carsen Taite. Two women fulfill their mutual desire with a night of passion, neither expecting more until law professor Morgan Bradley and student Parker Casey meet again…in the classroom. (978-1-60282-086-9)

Rough Trade edited by Todd Gregory. Top male erotica writers pen their own hot, sexy versions of the term "rough trade," producing some of the hottest, nastiest, and most dangerous fiction ever published. (978-1-60282-092-0)

The High Priest and the Idol by Jane Fletcher. Jemeryl and Tevi's relationship is put to the test when the Guardian sends Jemeryl on a mission that puts her not only in harm's way, but back into the sights of a previous lover. (978-1-60282-085-2)

Point of Ignition by Erin Dutton. Amid a blaze that threatens to consume them both, firefighter Kate Chambers and property owner Alexi Clark redefine love and trust. (978-1-60282-084-5)

Secrets in the Stone by Radclyffe. Reclusive sculptor Rooke Tyler suddenly finds herself the object of two very different women's affections, and choosing between them will change her life forever. (978-1-60282-083-8)

Dark Garden by Jennifer Fulton. Vienna Blake and Mason Cavender are sworn enemies—who can't resist each other. Something has to give. (978-1-60282-036-4)

Late in the Season by Felice Picano. Set on Fire Island, this is the story of an unlikely pair of friends—a gay composer in his late thirties and an eighteen-year-old schoolgirl. (978-1-60282-082-1)

Punishment with Kisses by Diane Anderson-Minshall. Will Megan find the answers she seeks about her sister Ashley's murder or will her growing relationship with one of Ash's exes blind her to the real truth? (978-1-60282-081-4)

September Canvas by Gun Brooke. When Deanna Moore meets TV personality Faythe she is reluctantly attracted to her, but will Faythe side with the people spreading rumors about Deanna? (978-1-60282-080-7)

No Leavin' Love by Larkin Rose. Beautiful, successful Mercedes Miller thinks she can resume her affair with ranch foreman Sydney Campbell, but the rules have changed. (978-1-60282-079-1)

Between the Lines by Bobbi Marolt. When romance writer Gail Prescott meets actress Tannen Albright, she develops feelings that she usually only experiences through her characters. (978-1-60282-078-4)

Blue Skies by Ali Vali. Commander Berkley Levine leads an elite group of pilots on missions ordered by her ex-lover Captain Aidan Sullivan and everything is on the line—including love. (978-1-60282-077-7)

The Lure by Felice Picano. When Noel Cummings is recruited by the police to go undercover to find a killer, his life will never be the same. (978-1-60282-076-0)

Death of a Dying Man by J.M. Redmann. Mickey Knight, Private Eye and partner of Dr. Cordelia James, doesn't need a drop-dead gorgeous assistant—not until nature steps in. (978-1-60282-075-3)

Justice for All by Radclyffe. Dell Mitchell goes undercover to expose a human traffic ring and ends up in the middle of an even deadlier conspiracy. (978-1-60282-074-6)

Sanctuary by I. Beacham. Cate Canton faces one major obstacle to her goal of crushing her business rival, Dita Newton—her uncontrollable attraction to Dita. (978-1-60282-055-5)

The Sublime and Spirited Voyage of Original Sin by Colette Moody. Pirate Gayle Malvern finds the presence of an abducted seamstress, Celia Pierce, a welcome distraction until the captive comes to mean more to her than is wise. (978-1-60282-054-8)

Suspect Passions by VK Powell. Can two women, a city attorney and a beat cop, put aside their differences long enough to see that they're perfect for each other? (978-1-60282-053-1)

Just Business by Julie Cannon. Two women who come together—each for her own selfish needs—discover that love can never be as simple as a business transaction. (978-1-60282-052-4)

Sistine Heresy by Justine Saracen. Adrianna Borgia, survivor of the Borgia court, presents Michelangelo with the greatest temptations of his life while struggling with soul-threatening desires for the painter Raphaela. (978-1-60282-051-7)